MURDER

IN THE FAMILY

THE AUDREY MURDERS

LEONIE MATEER

Murder in The Family
Copyright © 2016 by Leonie Mateer.

Published in the United States of America

Mystery/Crime/Fiction
Women's Fiction/Crime
4.22.2016

Paperback ISBN: 978-0-9976574-2-5
eBook ISBN: 978-0-9976574-3-2

I am dedicating this book to you, the reader ~

With gratitude for allowing me to share with you another story told

CHAPTER
ONE

Words. Nasty, hateful words. Recriminations, accusations, words written in spiny squiggles on yellowed paper – remnants from her diary. Ben closed the book and fell back on the pillow. *It's too late. I should never have kept it.* Her words burned holes in his mind. *I hope she burns in hell!*

As his thumb felt for each pearl in practiced formation, he recalled the last time she wore them. Her pale blue eyes shocked open, smeared red lips stretched, her swanlike neck straining against his clumsy hands as he watched her light fade and the pearls fall to the floor.

Retribution was imminent. He lowered the lid of her keep-sake box and closed his eyes. Each breath now more difficult. He hadn't left a will. No need. He had nothing left to give. His family hadn't spoken to him in years. He hadn't even bothered to leave them a farewell note. What was there to say? That he was sorry? That he was responsible for her death? It was too long ago.

He heard the door open and turned to face the wall.

CHAPTER
TWO

A udrey opened the email. She had red-flagged it earlier in the day knowing she would open it and read it when she had the courage to do so. What could her sisters want with her now? Too many years had passed. Too many words left unsaid.

There it was. In black and white. Just like them. No please or thank you. They were coming to stay at her cabins. All of them. Uninvited and unwanted. *Important,* she read. *We need to talk.* What could they possibly need to talk about that couldn't be done over the phone?

The cabins were all fully booked for the next few weeks. She would need to cancel reservations and suffer the financial loss. Damn her sisters!

It was mid-day. Most of the guests had already checked out. She picked up the phone and began to make the calls.

CHAPTER
THREE

Honey's suitcase was a jumbled disaster. What to wear? That was the question. Every year her suitcases got bigger and bigger to accommodate her ever-increasing clothes size. This trip wasn't her idea. It was bloody Becka's. She had called the meeting.

"It is time to sort this all out," she had said. "We have no choice."

Honey wished she had said no. But saying no to Becka was not that easy.

Honey picked up the heavy suitcase and dragged it downstairs. Fat, fluffy cats sat waiting in their cage. Honey hated taking them to the cattery as much as they hated staying there. Thank goodness it would only be for a few days. Her long skirt caught in the door as she slammed it shut, pissing her off even more. *Why do we have to bring it all up now?* She pulled at the skirt. *When I wanted to talk about it everyone acted as though it was all in my head.* She unlocked the door to release her skirt and dropped the keys. *Shit, shit, shit.* The cats meowed in unison protesting their confined quarters and lack of attention.

CHAPTER
FOUR

The wind pulled at her coat, exposing her to the bitter cold. The platform, eerily empty, filled with the roar of the approaching train. She pulled her suitcase up the steps and was welcomed with a blast of warm air. It was a fifteen-minute ride to Heathrow and a grueling twenty-hour flight to New Zealand.

How long since she had seen her sisters and brother? She couldn't count the years. They had been just children. Escaping to London in her late teens was the best thing Becka had ever done. She had made a life for herself. At least it **had** been a life. Now she was alone. Her husband was up north, remarried and affluent. Her sons were lawyers in the City. She hadn't told them about her trip. She wouldn't. They knew nothing of her past and never would.

How did the old woman get my phone number? she wondered. He was dying. *Well bloody good riddance!* It was not sympathy but pure curiosity that stirred her into action. Greta was adamant that she should come.

"He's going fast. I didn't know whom else to call. You were

the only family he ever talked about. He keeps saying he is sorry.*" Sorry for what?* "You had better come."

She would come. But she was not doing this alone. They were all involved. The doors swung open and she pushed her way passed the incoming passengers and up the escalators towards the terminal.

CHAPTER
FIVE

Audrey cancelled all her guests for the next five days. She didn't want strangers around her family. Best to keep things quiet. All the cabins were clean and ready for their arrival tomorrow. Tonight she would visit her brother, Ben. There could only be one reason for her sisters' sudden call to arms. She must make sure their secret remained a secret.

She parked her Rav4 off the road, out of sight and walked across the overgrown lawn toward the derelict villa. Old rusty bike wheels leaned against the front veranda – a reminder of her brother's healthier days. Wicker chairs, unwound and unloved, sat on either side of the front door. Audrey took the small path leading to the back door. Branches tore at her clothes as she made her way in the shadows. Peering in through the window she saw Greta stooped over the stove staring into a large black pot.

"What do you want?" she snapped, startled at Audrey's uninvited entrance.

"I think you're stirring up trouble. What have you been

saying? Whom have you been talking to? I thought we had an agreement," said Audrey.

"Been saying nothing." The old woman snapped.

"Where is my brother?"

"He's in his room. I wouldn't disturb him. He's sleeping."

Audrey pushed past the woman and made her way down the long hallway to her brother's bedroom. As she opened the door the pungent smell of death was overwhelming. She was too late. Her brother lay motionless. She felt for his pulse. Nothing. He was gone. Then she saw it. An ornate wooden box sat on his side table. She recognized it immediately. Why does he still have it? She opened it and let out a long sigh. There it was. The proof. She had told him to burn the diary long ago. He hadn't. Now she had a problem. Greta must have read it. Is that why her sisters were coming to stay?

She noticed Greta's bedroom door was ajar and peered into the stark, sparse space. A small table lamp exposed a single bed with white spread, a wooden chest of drawers, a wardrobe and a straight-backed chair as its sole contents. There was a suitcase on the bed. Audrey wondered if she was planning on going somewhere. Surely not. Approaching the suitcase she lifted the lid. It was packed. She opened a drawer in the dresser. Nothing. Greta knows, and she is leaving. But where to? To whom?

Audrey returned to the kitchen and sat down at the table. "He has gone," she told Greta.

Greta looked undisturbed at the news and remained staring into the pot as it came to a boil.

"Why don't you take a seat and let me make the tea," Audrey suggested graciously.

Greta removed two cups from the shelf above the stove and placed them on the bench. "It's no trouble," she said gruffly.

Audrey insisted. "Please, you have done so much for my

brother. The least I can do is make the tea." She turned the old lady gently towards the table in the center of the kitchen and reached for the tea caddy on the top shelf. "Did you contact Becka and Honey? You know you should have called me first."

The old lady looked guilty. "I phoned Becka because Ben was so upset. He kept calling her name. Seemed to want to tell her something before he died."

"What sort of things?" Audrey poured a splash of milk into both cups.

"I don't know. He didn't say. But I bet it had something to do with that old diary he kept reading over and over again."

"What diary? Did he show it to you?" Audrey asked

as she removed a tea bag from the tea caddy and another from her pocket, placed them in the cups and covered them with boiling water.

The old woman didn't answer.

"Did you read it?" Audrey carried both cups to the table and handed one to Greta.

"So what if I did?" she said. "What difference does it make now? He is dead." Greta sipped her tea and complained. "Didn't you add any sugar?"

Audrey collected the old china sugar bowl with a little macramé beaded cover and tiny sugar spoon and watched as Greta added multiple scoops of sugar to her tea.

Audrey knew she was going to have a busy night. In fifteen minutes Greta would be dead. Suicide, they would say. The old woman would no longer have had a roof over her head and nothing left to live for. At least, that is what Audrey would tell the police if they ever asked. She felt for Greta's pulse. It was weak. She picked up the cups and meticulously washed away all traces of their contents, emptied the pot of boiling water into the sink and returned everything to its appropriate place.

Stepping over the old lady crumpled at her feet, she revisited her brother's bedroom and collected every remaining piece of evidence she could find. The box, her mother's diary, newspaper clippings stuffed in files in his desk, the pearl necklace and his laptop computer.

She had one last task. Opening Greta's suitcase she removed every garment, one by one, and returned them, neatly folded, to their respective places in the drawers. Finding a one-way bus ticket to Auckland in Greta's old clasp purse, she tucked it into her pocket and placed the old suitcase on top of the wardrobe. She looked at her phone. They would be here soon. She had made the call after retrieving her car and parking it in the driveway. It was just on eleven thirty.

She fondled her mother's pearls now prettily adorning her own slender neck. They were exceptional in design. Each pearl perfectly sized. She sighed. They belonged to her now.

CHAPTER
SIX

Higgins had returned from walking his dog when his phone interrupted his nightly ritual. He was a meticulous man, one of the reasons he lived alone. Except for Marcus, of course. Marcus was a boxer breed, which meant he slobbered – a trait that Higgins had never come to terms with, and never would. But loyalty and responsibility were two of the detective's biggest attributes that, no doubt, explained his canine tolerance.

"Detective Constable Higgins," he barked into the phone.

"Yes, detective, we have a situation here. Two bodies. Don't like the look of it. 365 Mountain Road. Would like your opinion."

"Two bodies you say? I'm on my way. Don't touch a thing."

It was after midnight. Marcus liked to accompany him on his nightly rounds but tonight he would leave him at home. He didn't know how long this would take. The funeral directors only called him when they suspected foul play. He presumed the coroner would already be on his way.

The scene inside was quiet and orderly. The funeral

director had cordoned off the two areas where the dead lay undisturbed. The elderly lady's body was cold to the touch. The middle-aged man's body was in the early stages of rigor mortis indicating that he had been dead for at least three hours. He looked at the time, one a.m. He guessed the time of death to be around ten p.m. The lady, he couldn't tell. There were no signs of injury to either body. "Who called you?" he asked.

"Audrey Wetherby," replied the funeral director, looking at his notes. "She is waiting in the library. I thought you would want to speak with her, so I asked her to stay. She said the man is her brother and the old lady is his caregiver. Her brother was diagnosed with stage-four brain cancer. His death was imminent and expected. The old lady's death is a mystery."

Higgins used his cell phone to snap a few photos of both bedrooms and the kitchen area before entering the library.

The blonde middle-aged woman stood up when he approached.

"Detective Constable Higgins," he introduced himself. "I am sorry for your loss. Please sit down."

"Thank you, detective." Her voice soft and purposeful. "He was my brother. He was in such pain and is in a better place now."

"Tell me about the lady? I understand she was his caregiver."

"She has been with him for fifteen years or so. She was his housekeeper until he became ill. Then she became his caregiver. Maybe it was the shock of him passing that caused her death. I know they were very close. She was like his mother."

"Are your parents still alive?" he asked.

"No, our parents passed away many years ago."

"Do you know if Greta has any living relatives? Anyone we should contact?"

"No-one that I know of. This was her home. I have already given the funeral directors all the information they asked for.

"Your brother, any children?"

"My brother never married. He was very reclusive. There is just myself and my three sisters."

"Thank you," said the detective. "It is late and I'm sure you want to get home. I just need to take your details in case I need further information."

Audrey obliged, handing him a set of keys to the old villa. "Can you please lock up when you have finished and put the keys under the mat by the back door?"

"One last thing. Did Greta have any health problems that you know of?"

"She had a weak heart but refused to see any doctors," Audrey stood up to leave. "At least that is what my brother told me. She was a strange old woman. A spinster who liked my brother's reclusive environment. They were well suited, my brother and she."

"Oh, one more thing, sorry. How did you come to be here? I presume they were both dead when you arrived?"

"Yes, Detective. They were both dead. It was just a coincidence. I came to visit my brother. I knew he was desperately ill. Unfortunately I was too late. I would have liked to have said a final goodbye."

The detective shared the news with the coroner. "The old lady had a weak ticker, it would appear."

"Looks like we have two deaths as the result of natural causes." The coroner removed his gloves and picked up his bag. "You can take them away," he advised the funeral directors. He looked at Higgins. "I will fill out the paperwork and get you a copy first thing in the morning."

"Sorry to get you out of bed" the funeral director said to Higgins. "Looks like I need not have bothered you."

"No worries. Appreciate the call. I would have done the same thing."

As he walked toward his car he thought it odd that Ms. Wetherby just happened to arrive not long after they had died. And both of them dying within a few hours of each other? Higgins didn't like coincidences.

Something was bugging the detective. As he pulled into his driveway he remembered what it was. The home of Ben Brown was immaculate – everything in its place except for a suitcase in the old woman's room. It was sitting at an uncomfortable angle atop the wardrobe. Anyone who is so precise in his or her neatness would never position it in that manner. Higgins would know, suffering himself from borderline OCD. The angle of the suitcase would be a constant irritation. Also, in the kitchen, every plate, cup and spoon had their designated home with the exception of two china cups on a shelf. Their handles faced in the opposite direction from the rest of the matching set. A tea caddy and sugar bowl also looked somewhat disturbed. He doubted the old lady had put them there. Mr. Brown was obviously unable to make tea in the kitchen. So who placed the cups on the shelf? Had someone else made tea in the kitchen recently? There was also a small printer in the library but no sign of a computer. Why?

Marcus rushed to the door to greet him. "Missed me, didn't you old boy?" Marcus knew not to jump up on his owner. He wagged his tail and gave a short bark.

It was good to be home.

CHAPTER
SEVEN

I t was bedlam in the Mayflower home. Piper was pulling clothes out of drawers hunting for her favorite blue top with the cut-out sleeves. Her mother was yelling constantly, telling her they had to leave for the airport in thirty minutes. It was a school day and she was chuffed she was missing the geometry test. Her friends were so jealous she was going to Northland with her parents and wouldn't be back until Tuesday next week.

"I'm definitely surfing at Taupo Bay and snorkeling and waterskiing," she had responded to their endless questions. Of course she didn't tell them the main reason for their trip was to attend her Uncle Ben's funeral. She had never met him. He was the uncle no-one talked about.

"I'm coming," she called for the umpteenth time.

"Your father is already in the car." Her mother looked agitated. "I hope you packed something suitable for the funeral?"

CHAPTER
EIGHT

A udrey stood waiting at the Kerikeri airport. Becka was arriving any minute from London. She was not looking forward to seeing her sister. Becka was the cold one – detached and demanding. She wasn't even the oldest. But somehow had taken on the role of everyone's keeper. Not that the sisters communicated often. Audrey tried to remember the last time she had seen Becka. It was on one of her trips to London. That was years ago.

Passengers descended from the small plane and walked in single file across the tarmac to the small arrivals area. Audrey watched intently as every female came into view. She heard her before she saw her: "Audrey, you haven't changed a bit. Still have a good appetite I see." *Yep. Nothing has changed.*

"Hi," she responded. "Welcome to sunny Northland. You must be dying to get out of all those black heavy clothes. Here, let me take your suitcase." The offer was partly necessitated by the frail frame of her half-starved sister and partly by the role she automatically assumed when luggage was involved. Even guests would watch politely as Audrey carried their suitcases, implying it perfectly acceptable to have a middle-aged woman assume the role of porter.

Once in the car and heading north, Becka began a barrage of questions: "Did you get a chance to talk to Ben before he died? What the hell happened to Greta? Have you organized everything for the funeral? Are we responsible for Greta's funeral too? Does she have any family? Audrey answered best she could under the circumstances. "We have an appointment at the funeral home tomorrow to go over all the final details," she said.

"Has Honey arrived yet?" Becka wanted to know. Audrey nodded.

"I haven't seen her for donkey's years. How does she look? She was always Dad's favorite. He used to take her everywhere." Becka looked out the window at the rolling green hills. "It is so great to be home. I had forgotten how beautiful it is here. It is so cold in London. " She removed her wool scarf and unbuttoned her jacket. "Maybe I will stay in New Zealand, there is really nothing to go back to."

Horrors, thought Audrey. "You would miss city life," she responded.

"I guess so. I do live a cultured lifestyle. London is such a cosmopolitan city. I would miss the theater, concerts, art galleries, museums, restaurants…." Becka yawned. "I am absolutely exhausted."

"We will be there soon. Why don't you lie back and take a nap?"

Becka didn't take much convincing. The forty-minute drive back to Hihi was pleasantly silent, except for her sister's occasional ladylike snore.

CHAPTER
NINE

The man stood back from the crowd at the burial site. He hadn't known his aunt very well. He had seen the notice in the paper:

Whangarei. Greta Baywater died Wednesday, 17th February 2016 at the home of Ben Brown where she was a long-time resident and caregiver.
Born in 1938, Greta was a professional nurse, housekeeper and caregiver during her many years of community service.
She was a very private person who enjoyed crossword puzzles, hymns and knitting, often donating garments she knitted to the Salvation Army. She was an avid churchgoer and regularly played the organ at the Whangarei Baptist Church.
The Whangarei Funeral Service has been

entrusted with arrangements.

He didn't know how she had died but presumed it was by natural causes. However, her death was a surprise as he had just received a letter from her, asking if she could come and visit him. The request had sounded urgent. He was her only living relative. By the time he received news of her death, the family of Ben Brown had already made the funeral arrangements. He didn't want to intrude. He was surprised so many people had turned up at her funeral.

"Are you a relative?" Startled by the man standing behind him, he swung to face him. "Sorry, I didn't mean to intrude. I'm Detective Constable Higgins. I was wondering if you were a relative of Greta Baywater's?" he repeated.

"I am her nephew, Matt Walters," he responded.

"Did you know her well?" the detective asked.

"Actually, no. I haven't seen Aunt Greta for years. Funny though, I just received a letter from her asking if she could come stay with me. Do you know how she died?"

"Natural causes as far as we can tell. I understand she had a bad heart. The shock of Ben Brown's dying must have been too much for her."

"Ben Brown is dead? When did he die?"

"The same night. He died only a few hours before your aunt died."

"Strange. In her letter she wrote it was urgent she leave the house. She sounded almost afraid. She asked if she could stay with me for a while."

"Do you still have the letter?"

"I do." He reached into his pocket, extracted a small pink envelope and handed it to the detective.

Removing the hand-written note, Higgins read:

Dear Matt,

I know it has been a long while since we had the pleasure of dining at your dear Mother's house before she passed away. I miss her so and think of her often.

I do hope this letter finds you in good health.

A situation has arisen and I find myself in need of temporary accommodation. I must leave immediately and would be most grateful if I could visit with you for a few days until I can find new lodgings.

I plan on taking the 7 p.m. bus to Auckland on Thursday and will telephone you upon my arrival.

Yours gratefully,

Greta Baywater

"When she didn't turn up at the bus terminal, I was worried. I didn't have her telephone number and it wasn't until I saw the notice in the paper that I realized what had happened." Matt explained.

"Mind if I take a copy of the letter?" The detective said as he folded it and placed it in the envelope.

"Why. Do you think her death is suspicious? You said it was her heart."

"Most likely she died from natural causes but I would like to do some more investigating."

"I am staying at the Casa De La Vista on Tui Street. You can return the letter to me there. Do you know anyone from Ben Brown's family? I would like to thank them for handling all of Greta's funeral arrangements.

The detective looked at the dispersing crowd and pointed to Audrey Wetherby. "The lady with the red scarf is Ben's sister. She found your aunt and her brother on the night they died. Let me introduce you."

CHAPTER
TEN

A udrey saw the detective walking toward her with a man she didn't recognize. "Ms. Wetherby, let me introduce Matt Walters. He is Greta Baywater's nephew." The man held out his hand and shook hers with a strong determined grasp.

"Thank you for looking after all the funeral arrangements. Please, let me reimburse you for the trouble." He reached in his pocket and removed a card and handed it to her.

Audrey took the card without looking at it. "It was no trouble. Greta was like family to us. She took care of my brother for over fifteen years. It was the least we could do for her." She looked intently at the well-dressed man in front of her. "We were unaware Greta had any family."

"I should have been there for her. I travel extensively and have been over in Europe for many years and just returned a few months ago. In fact, I received a letter from Greta requesting to come and stay with me. Such a shame we left it too late to reconnect. I am sorry for your loss. I understand your brother also passed away."

Audrey was preoccupied. *A letter. Greta wrote him a letter? Was that why her suitcase was packed? Why she had a one-way ticket to Auckland? What had she written?* "Yes, his funeral is tomorrow. He was very sick. We will miss him terribly."

"I would like to pick up my aunt's belongs if that is alright. I don't want to cause more work for you, but she is all the family I had and there might be some things I can keep as mementoes."

Audrey's mind was spinning. "Yes, of course. I packed them in boxes and they are in storage at Tiromoana in Hihi. If you stop by after Ben's funeral tomorrow afternoon we are having tea on the lawn at three. Just take the road past the Hihi motor camp and up Peninsula road. Tiromoana is the first entranceway on the left. You are welcome to join us. She looked at the detective. "You are also invited." It was a half-hearted invitation but she figured he would attend Ben's funeral anyway. He was such a nosey son of a bitch. She needed to keep an eye on him.

The men moved towards the graveside as Audrey stumbled across the cemetery lawn in her inappropriate high heels. *Bloody men. Now I have to go to Ben's and nose around the villa.* She stopped to remove her shoe that was firmly stuck in the dirt. *Bloody hell!*

CHAPTER
ELEVEN

Piper let out a whistle. "Wow, this is where Audrey lives? It's fantastic."

A sign, 'Tiromoana' painted white on native wood and nailed to a tree marked the entrance to six cabins and Audrey's cottage overlooking Doubtless Bay. Tall pine trees swayed in the warm sea breeze as the family headed down the long gravel driveway towards the opening to the ocean.

As they pulled into the car park Simone gasped. "Oh my God! What a view!"

Becka and Honey were spread out on the lawn like brown bunnies. They turned when the car approached and waved.

"Oh Mum, this is great! I'm going to go swimming immediately."

Simone and John removed their luggage from the rental car and headed towards the cottage while Piper ran to her aunties and fell down dramatically beside them. "I'm Piper," she said. "You must be my wonderful aunties whom I have never met."

Audrey was in the office. She looked completely shocked to see her oldest sister and her husband standing in front of her. "I didn't think you were coming," she said. "Becka and Honey thought you both had work commitments."

"That was before Ben actually died. I didn't want to get involved in a pointless family discussion about things in the past. But of course we would come to his funeral. He was, after all, my brother." Simone looked hurt.

Audrey grabbed a key and walked with them to the Morepork Cabin on the far ridge overlooking Hihi harbor. It was the largest of all the cabins and would easily accommodate all three of them. She had watched their teenage daughter join her sisters on the lawn and envied her youth and vibrancy. Two attributes Audrey could no longer claim as her own.

For tonight she planned a BBQ on the front lawn. Becka had made a spinach and caper salad. Honey was responsible for desert and had magically produced a combination of fluff and puff delights. Her sisters had already started on the wine and were on their second bottle by the time Audrey returned from Ben's with a carload of Greta's possessions.

During the packing process, Audrey had discovered another side to Greta. She professed to be a good Christian and had half a dozen bibles to prove it – and yet, it would appear, she had a morbid interest in the occult. Books with titles including the words: *Magic*, *Witchcraft*, *Demonology*, *Wicca* and *Tarot* were stacked in boxes under her bed. Audrey found a diary containing dates of psychic readings complete with names and dates of clients. What the hell? Greta was a fortune-teller? She laughed. Shame she couldn't predict her own fate. Looking through the entries, Audrey realized that Greta had kept a record of her clients' secret fears and past indiscretions. She searched for an entry about her brother, Ben. Her heart stopped beating as she read the lines about her brother's truths and regrets. Greta knew. Greta knew everything. The last entry had been written the day her brother died. Had Greta told anyone what she knew? Her nephew, perhaps?

Audrey placed Greta's bibles and her bland, matronly outfits neatly into cardboard boxes for her nephew to collect tomorrow. She made sure she included some jewelry and a few select novels and biographies from her literary collection. Her nephew would believe his aunt had been a nice, god-fearing woman. Now, this was not an attempt to put Greta's memory in a good light, but rather to avoid any lingering interest in the woman. The other, more interesting items, she placed in a box and marked it carefully, "Ben's books."

CHAPTER
TWELVE

Honey was dressed to kill. She had an opinion about funerals. They were a time of remembrance and celebration and the color black had nothing to do with either. She wouldn't expose her ample cleavage as a point of respect but a wide-brimmed hat, a tight-fitting bodice and hip-hugging polka-dot skirt worked perfectly with her new red shoes. Now, if a nice single man just happened to be at the funeral, that would really top off the occasion. There was nothing Honey liked better than men – except, of course, for Mr. Fluffy and Tinkers.

Last night had been really strange. She had spent the afternoon getting sloshed with Becka while Audrey ran around like a chicken with her head cut off having insisted on attending Greta's funeral. Honey felt that paying for the bloody funeral was good enough. "Ben would have wanted that," Audrey had insisted. Then later her sister returned with a carload of Greta's belongings, saying her nephew was collecting it all after Ben's funeral. Bloody hell, who knew the old lady had a nephew?

When Simone, John and Piper arrived, it was pretty much a

full house of strangers pretending they were family. Or was it the other way round? Whatever it was, it was a disaster. No-one wanted to talk about Ben or dredge up the past. They were all in bed by nine o'clock.

The funeral home in Kerikeri had arranged for cars to pick them up. Honey, Becka and Audrey piled into the first car. Simone and family into the second. It was a private event. They had avoided putting his death notice in the newspaper for fear that someone from their past should spot it. By tonight it would all be behind them. Ben would be six feet under and they could return to their busy lives.

"Honey Brown?" Honey turned to see a ghost from the past staring at her. He hadn't changed a bit. Still tall, gaunt and reeking of booze and tobacco. "Uncle Steve! What a surprise. I didn't expect to see you here. I thought you had moved to Australia. How is Aunt Betty? Is she here too?" Honey looked around and caught Becka's eye. Becka looked shocked when she saw whom Honey was talking to and walked over to join them.

"My wife passed away many years ago. Goodness gracious, is that you Becka? My, you have grown into a beautiful woman. Are you still in London? Ben told me you're married."

"I didn't know you were in contact with Ben?" Becka was shocked.

"I wasn't until a few days ago. His housekeeper called me and said that Ben was in distress and wanted to talk to me. During our conversation he mentioned that you had moved to London and married an artist. A painter, I understand?"

Their conversation was cut short as Audrey approached the group. "Uncle Steve, I see you made the funeral. I thought you and my brother were not on speaking terms."

"We are family." The old man looked uncomfortable at the accusation.

"You must join us for afternoon tea at Audrey's," Becka offered awkwardly. "It's only a forty-minute drive from here. Here, let me give you the address in case you get lost." *Or want to stop at a pub or two on the way.*

"Thank you, I think I will," he looked at Audrey. "We need to have a talk, you and me."

Audrey knew her father and Uncle Steve had a falling-out shortly after a young girl's body had been found on the stony banks of the local Waimakariri River. The police had interviewed her father as a person of interest in the girl's murder. But Audrey had always wondered if it was her uncle who had committed the crime. A car was spotted at the scene that matched the description of her father's Hillman Hunter. The neighbors had reported him to the police when he was seen changing the color of the car shortly after the body had been found. She remembered her uncle borrowing the car and going fishing the day the girl was killed. No-one was ever held responsible for the crime. She always knew they had had something to do with it.

Audrey wondered what her uncle wanted to talk to her about. She worried about what Ben may have said to him.

Too many secrets left unspoken. Had her uncle learned something that implicated Audrey? Is that why he wanted to talk to her?

CHAPTER
THIRTEEN

etective Constable Higgins looked on from afar as the family stood at the graveside. Who was that woman in the big hat? He guessed she was one of the sisters. He watched as the group walked away from the grave in silence and returned to the waiting cars. An elderly, unkempt man remained. Higgins walked over to him and introduced himself. "Detective Constable Higgins. I am sorry for your loss. A friend of yours?"

"He was my nephew, my brother's son. Steve Brown," he introduced himself.

The detective was standing downwind of the man and turned to avoid the stench of alcohol. "Were you close?"

"We hadn't talked in years. That is, until a few days ago. He was extremely distraught, wanted to talk about my brother's death – terrible thing. But, I'm sure you know all about that. What with the case still being open."

Detective Higgins had no idea what he was referring to but didn't miss a beat. "Wanted to get something off his chest before he died, did he?"

"Oh, it was nothing important. Just family stuff." The man replied obviously regretting his indiscretion.

"Gotta go. Audrey is having some sort of reception at her place and I'm invited. Never miss a free drink and a feed."

The detective followed the man back to the car park and tried to press him for more information, but to no avail. Although he was also invited, he had no intention of attending the reception. Instead, he began making calls. "I want a search on Ben Brown, his family, everything. Now!" he shouted into the phone. *Damn, I knew there was more to these deaths.*

CHAPTER
FOURTEEN

hit, shit, shit. Audrey was pissed off. She sat in the back of the sedan next to her sisters in silence. What the hell was he doing here? What the fuck did Ben tell him? Now the shithead wanted to talk to her. About what? Did he know? Surely not? Ben promised no matter what, he would never tell anyone who'd been there that night – least of all Uncle Steve, the drunken bastard.

As they pulled into her car park, she saw Greta's nephew, Matt, waiting in his car staring out at the view across the bay. Simone and family pulled in behind them. As the sisters poured out of the cars in unison, Matt walked over to greet them.

Audrey now had two troublemakers on hand. *Keep your friends close and your enemies closer.* "Matt, glad you could make it. I have Greta's belongings all ready for you. Please stay and have a drink with us. It has been a long day and you must be tired. Grab a seat at the table on the front lawn. Wine or beer? What would you like?"

"A beer would be great," he said, as he walked with her sisters to the picnic tables.

Piper followed her aunty inside. "Let me help you Aunty Audrey."

"Thanks Piper. Can you carry out the sandwiches and a couple bottles of wine? I will bring out the beer and glasses."

Audrey handed a beer to Matt while her sisters opened the wine. The sun was still high in the sky. Simone's husband, John, raised the umbrellas. Piper passed around the food. A happy family gathering, one would think. Audrey knew otherwise.

This family had serious problems. Problems that should have been resolved with Ben and Greta's deaths. *Damn, Greta – now you have involved your nephew and I will have to take care of it.*

Audrey watched her sisters with envy. They all seemed so sure of who they were. Even Honey, the eccentric one, had a firm grip on her reality. She was making a play for Matt. Give Honey a whiff of testosterone and she is divinely happy.

Honey smiled at her. "Audrey, why doesn't Matt stay here tonight?"

"He is most welcome," Audrey turned at the sound of another car crunching down the gravel driveway. It was Uncle Steve. Tonight she would need to find out just how much these two men knew. She knew her Uncle Steve was an easy mark. He would spout his head off after a bottle of whisky, and whisky she had aplenty. He would be too drunk to drive home.

She walked over to greet him. "Uncle Steve, you made it. Come join us."

CHAPTER
FIFTEEN

He looked at the time. It was six o'clock. He had been at his computer for hours. Why the hell hadn't he done the search before the bodies were buried? There it was, in black and white, a newspaper article from thirty years ago.

A photo of Mr. and Mrs. Brown featured prominently on the front page of *The Christchurch Star*. They looked like a nice, ordinary couple. Mrs. Brown was wearing a twin set and pearls. The article read:

> A brother and sister are now classified as 'persons of interest' regarding their parents' sudden deaths.
> Christchurch lay preacher and truck driver, Murray Brown and his wife, Sophie, were found dead at their Northcote home on Saturday night. Mr. Brown had suffered multiple stab wounds and

his wife's death was a result of stran-
gulation.
"We have no suspects at this time,"
said Detective Constable Williams, the
lead detective on the case. "We are
questioning all members of the family
and anyone who had contact with the
Browns prior to their death."
When asked about the brother and his
sister being
questioned for many hours yesterday,
the detective stated, "As already
mentioned, we are questioning all
members of the family. Two members of
the family are helping us with our
enquiries, but no arrests have been
made at this time."

Higgins went on to read article after article until he had exhausted every piece of public evidence relating to the case. What interested him the most was the fact it was an unsolved case. No-one had been brought to justice. It was not thought to have been a robbery. There was no forced entry into the home. Multiple stabbings and strangulation indicated a crime of passion. Personal even.

The children's names were suppressed due to their age. He needed to get hold of all the files in cold storage. He picked up the phone and ordered the files be sent to his Whangarei office first thing in the morning. The son must have been Ben, but which sister was the suspect?

This morning he had returned the letter to the old lady's nephew at the motel. He had caught him as he was checking out. "Decided to stay further up North. I am picking up my aunt's belongings from Audrey's place in Hihi." Matt Walters stuffed the letter in his pocket. Higgins wondered if Walters and Paul Brown were still at Audrey's. He checked the time. Damn. It was a two-hour drive to Hihi. They would be well gone before he could get there. He left a message for Matt suggesting they meet tomorrow morning.

CHAPTER
SIXTEEN

att looked at the women around him. All so different. Honey was a load of fun. He had agreed to spend the night. He really didn't have anywhere else to be and Tiromoana was just what he needed. Some peace and quiet, surrounded by native bush and open sea.

Life had taken many unexpected turns. His careers were as diverse as his interests. An engineer, a professor of mathematics and, until a few months ago, he had traveled Europe as a photographer. Even had some photos published in *National Geographic*. Honey said she wanted to see some of his work and was viewing it on his laptop with squeals of appreciation.

"Audrey, is it possible for me to collect my aunt's belongings?" He turned to face his hostess as she joined them on the lawn.

"I have already put them in the Kiwi Cabin for you," she said, as she handed him the keys. "You can park your car by the cabin. It's the second one on the ridge."

"Great. If you don't mind, I have a couple of calls to make."

The detective had been calling him but he had ignored his

calls until now. As soon as he had settled into the cabin, he returned the call.

"Detective, Matt Walters here, you have been trying to reach me? Oh, I see. Yes, I am at Audrey's now. I am staying in one of her cabins tonight … Yes, he is here too. Audrey was kind enough to accommodate us both. Tomorrow at eleven? I'll tell him. See you then."

I wonder what has stirred his interest, thought Matt. He opened the first box and started to sort through his aunt's keepsakes. Sad, it was. Just a few boxes of cheap jewelry, a few books, worn-out shoes and at least a dozen handbags. He removed a small heart-shaped pendant on a silver chain and a threadbare bible and lay them on the coffee table. The other boxes contained mostly clothes – old lady clothes. He would stop by a Salvation Army store on his way back to Auckland tomorrow and donate everything.

He heard a knock. Expecting the buxom Honey, he closed the last box and headed for the door. Audrey asked, "Can I come in for a moment?"

"Yes, by all means." Matt was surprised at the intrusion. She had been cold and politely distant since they had met. He didn't like the woman. So different from her sisters. He wondered what she could possibly want.

"Just checking everything is OK. I put a bottle of wine in your fridge. Please help yourself. We are having dinner at seven." Audrey appeared preoccupied with the boxes on the floor.

"Everything is great. Thank you. Do you know where the nearest Salvation Army store is? I would like to donate my aunt's clothes. I can drop them off when I leave tomorrow.

"There is a donation depot just down the road in

Mangonui. You can't miss it. There is a sign as you take the exit. So you are heading back to Auckland tomorrow?"

"That is the plan. Do you know where your uncle is? Detective Higgins called and wishes to meet with us both tomorrow at eleven." Did he imagine it or did Audrey flinch at the information?

Audrey smiled her perfect smile. "I will tell him. Are you meeting him here?" He nodded. "I will see you at dinner then – just a casual dinner on the lawn. It's such a beautiful night."

He watched through the cabin window as she walked to the cabin on the far side of the ridge. How did she know he lived in Auckland? He had never mentioned it. He noticed she was carrying a bottle of whisky. He watched as her uncle opened the door and she disappeared inside. "She's a strange one, that woman," he muttered to himself as he lay a clean pair of jeans and a button-down shirt on the bed and turned on the shower. Maybe Honey and he could hang out after dinner. He liked that woman. She was a little on the plump side, and he liked that.

CHAPTER
SEVENTEEN

B ecka was worried. Audrey had just joined her in the kitchen with the news the detective was coming there tomorrow to talk to Matt and Uncle Steve.

"What can he possibly want to talk to them about? After all, Ben was deathly ill and died naturally. Greta was just old and tired. Surely he doesn't suspect anyone?" Then her face froze. "You don't suppose they suspect Ben of killing the old lady before he died?"

"Don't be silly, Becka. Ben was too weak to even move at the end. There is no way he could have committed murder," Audrey soothed her sister's fears.

"He's done it before, she muttered silently.

"What did you say?" Audrey dropped two live crayfish into a large pot of boiling water. She listened for the scream. She knew the sound was only from gasses being released from under the lobster tail but she listened for it anyway. "He's done what before?"

"Nothing." Becka wiped her hands on the tea towel hanging

on the oven door. "I just don't want him to start bringing up things from the past."

"Don't you worry, Becka. That is long forgotten.

Anyway, what could Ben's death have to do with our parents' death? They never proved he had anything to do with it. They said he was home at the time but we know he was at work when it happened. He was doing deliveries. Remember? Anyway, we were all teenagers then. You were only seventeen. I was fifteen. Poor Honey was only twelve."

"Has Simone talked about it?" Becka wanted to know.

"No, she changes the subject every time I try to mention it. She had already left home for teachers college when it happened. She lives in constant denial of the whole thing. She acts as though Mum and Dad are still alive and enjoying their retirement somewhere. You know Simone; life is one big happy family."

"Do you think Honey knows anything?" Becka finished tossing the salad and removed the bread rolls from the oven.

"I don't think so. Why would she? She was playing with friends in the park across the street and has always insisted she didn't hear or see anything."

"What about you, Audrey? You have never told the police where you were that night. Why wouldn't you say?"

Audrey removed the bright orange crayfish from the pot with large tongs and placed them on a vibrant fish-shaped platter. "It was none of their business. The police were shits at the time – accusing us of murdering our parents. They had no proof. I'm glad you could avoid all the horrible accusations and constant allegations. Going to London was the best thing you could have done."

"But I left it all to you to handle, Audrey. I shouldn't have done that," Becka confessed.

"It's OK, Becka. It was thirty years ago. We have all got on with our lives. You have two beautiful grown sons and have a good life over there. I am sure Ben would not have wanted us to delve into the past." She handed Becka a glass of wine. "Drink up. Let's spend a nice evening together."

They gathered up the food and carried it across the lawn to the waiting guests. Honey was already sitting next to Matt, totally absorbed in conversation. Simone, John and Piper were playing cricket on the lawn.

"Dinner's served," called Audrey as she placed the crayfish on the table. "Piper, be a dear and grab the serviettes and cutlery from the kitchen. Oh, and bring another bottle of wine."

"Will do," obliged Piper. "Where is Uncle Steve? Isn't he joining us?"

"I'll go and check on him," Simone offered graciously. "He has most likely passed out. He drank a lot of wine this afternoon."

Audrey watched her walk toward the Tui Cabin. She set a place for him at the table. Her conversation with her uncle had not gone well earlier. He told her Ben had confessed to killing her mother. A "deathbed confession", he had called it. The drunk old man went on and on and on about how Ben had hated his parents. And how Ben had said he had not killed his father. Said it was one of his sisters. He accused Audrey.

Audrey couldn't take it any longer. She was prepared for what she needed to do. Just the right amount of GHB in his bottle of whisky would do the trick. He was an old man. Shame he had to die in one of her cabins, but it couldn't be helped. She couldn't risk him talking to the detective tomorrow. She really had no choice.

She waited until the old man couldn't hold his glass. She

took it from him, wiped off her fingerprints and placed it on the table. It was almost as though he knew. With his last drunken breath he said, "Ya know, it wasn't ya dad that killed that young girl. It was I." Audrey left the cabin reveling in deserved retribution.

"I can't wake him," said Simone, running across the lawn toward them. "He is hardly breathing. We need to call 111."

"I'll do it," said John. He looked at the screen then immediately handed his phone to Audrey. "You do it. You can give them directions."

It took over half an hour for the ambulance to arrive. They put Uncle Steve on a stretcher and headed off into the night, sirens blaring and lights flashing.

Matt Walters watched the commotion in silence. He wondered why no-one had accompanied their uncle to the hospital. He guessed Uncle Steve was not a family favorite. They returned to the dinner table and Audrey served a homemade apple sponge with runny cream. As the night wore on and the wine flowed, everyone began to relax. At midnight Audrey's phone rang. It was the hospital. Uncle Steve was dead. Died of a heart attack, they said.

Audrey sighed as she lifted her glass. "To Uncle Steve, may he rest in peace."

"To Uncle Steve," they toasted in unison.

CHAPTER
EIGHTEEN

I t was almost nine o'clock when Matt stirred. He turned to face the pretty woman by his side. He really liked her. She was fun and sexy at the same time. He didn't feel like returning to Auckland. He would much rather take Honey on a road trip. He texted the detective. *"Sorry can't make our meeting today, something has come up."* He chuckled.

"Good morning, handsome," Honey stretched like a cat waking from a dreamless sleep. "Wanna play today?"

"Thought we would take a trip up north to Cape Reinga. You up for it?"

"I thought you said you had a meeting?"

"Just cancelled it. We can grab an early lunch on the way." His phone beeped. It was a message from the detective. *"Please meet today. I have new information re your aunt's death."*

He responded, *"Let's meet tomorrow,"* turned off his phone and joined Honey in the shower. Whatever the detective had to say could wait. His aunt had been an old lady with a weak heart. A God-fearing spinster. She'd died of natural causes. What could the detective possibly have to add to that?

God, Honey has a great body, he thought as he soaped her voluptuous breasts with Eco soap. It was going to be a wonderful day.

CHAPTER
NINETEEN

etective Constable Higgins had woken to the news of Steve Brown's death. He had been up all night creating a crime wall in his office. Each Brown family member prominently positioned, in chronological order.

Murray & Sophie Brown – murdered when in their 40s. (Unsolved cold case)
Ben Brown – single – oldest child, only son – 20 at time of parents' death (Died of natural causes at 52)
Simone Mayflower – oldest daughter – 19 at time of parents' death
Becka Simpson – divorced? – second-oldest daughter – 17 at time of parents' death
Audrey Wetherby – divorced – third-oldest daughter – 15 at time of parents' death
Honey Brown – single – youngest daughter – 12 at time of parents' death
Steve Brown – brother of Murray Brown – 73 at time of death (died of natural causes?)

Greta Baywater – Ben Brown's housekeeper and care-
taker – 72 at time of death – (died of natural causes?)

Two deaths thirty years ago, and now three deaths in one
week. All related to the one family. Ben Brown's death was the
result of advanced brain cancer. Steve Brown and Greta
Baywater both documented as having died of natural causes –
or had they? Both died when Audrey Wetherby was in close
proximity. Both held the answers to an unsolved crime. A crime
in which Ms. Wetherby may well have been a suspect.

Scrutiny of Audrey Wetherby was very revealing. Murders
hovered around her like flies around a hot woolly sheep, yet she
had only ever been a person of interest. Her parents' death was
brutal and unexplained. A nice respectable couple with religious
morals and no apparent enemies. Ben, the oldest son was the
prime suspect but was never convicted. Was Audrey also a
suspect? She had no confirmed alibi, but there was no concrete
evidence. It was all circumstantial.

Higgins knew Steve Brown had had a conversation with
Ben before he died. Did Ben make a confession? A confession
that had gotten the old man murdered? Did Greta, the caregiver, also find out the truth? Was she, too, murdered to stop
her talking?

Who stood to gain from their deaths? It had to be Audrey
Wetherby. She was certainly quick to put the old lady in the
ground. Took full charge of the funeral arrangements. He
guessed she would have had her cremated if Greta's church had
not insisted she be buried.

He knew he had to talk to Greta's nephew, Matt. Maybe
there was a diary or notebook in which she'd kept her secrets.
When he called the coroner for an autopsy report, he was told
no autopsy had taken place as her death was due to natural

causes – her heart had simply given up. The detective wished he had had a toxicology report done before she was put in the ground. He would need some sort of proof she'd been murdered before he would get permission to dig her up. Damn!!

His phone rang. "Yes, I am familiar with Greta Baywater's death. I see. She was a psychic, you say? You had readings with her often. She foresaw her own death? I understand. Thank you. I will let you know if I need further information." *Crazy woman!*

He noticed he had a message. It was from Matt Walters, saying he couldn't make the meeting today. Damn! He really needed to meet with him.

He looked at the time. It was nine o'clock already. He lifted the lid off the big cold case box. Maybe there was some DNA he could test. Tomorrow he would head up to Tiromoana.

CHAPTER
TWENTY

Audrey was pacing. Things were out of her control and she didn't like it one bit. Uncle Steve's demise was unfortunate. Not that he didn't deserve what he got. He was always a dirty old man, just like his brother. But unfortunate in the sense she had had to take care of business in her own back yard. Three deaths in one week and a damn detective sniffing around.

She called her sister's cell. "Honey, have you seen Matt? I see. I thought he had a meeting with that detective today. Oh, really? Well, have a great time. I'll see you both tonight maybe."

So the meeting was off. Great news! Audrey took the first deep breath of the day. Now she had time to think. The meeting must not take place. Ever.

Becka, Simone, John and Piper had all left for a day at Whangaroa harbor. A day of boating, water skiing and fishing. Audrey was left in charge of arranging Uncle Steve's bloody funeral. This time she could insist on cremation. The funeral was scheduled for tomorrow. Closed casket, private ceremony and no announcement in the paper.

Audrey pulled out the box of Greta's belongings she had kept, and began to sort through the contents. Her notebooks were full of clients' names with corresponding personal data. An hour later Audrey sat back in stunned silence. Obviously Greta had not planned on dying so soon. She had her own box of secrets. Secrets she wouldn't want anyone to know. Who would have suspected the frail old woman of blackmail? But it was all there in black and white – she had been blackmailing her clients. What's more, there was over two hundred thousand dollars in her bank account. Deposits corresponding with entries in her notebook. Greta, you cunning old fox. The whole town must be pleased you are six feet under.

She knew she was covered. If any suspicion ever fell on her, she had proof that any one of Greta's psychic-reading seeking clients could have taken their revenge. Audrey poured herself another glass of wine and raided the fridge in celebration. Nothing like having ammunition in her back pocket for a rainy day.

CHAPTER
TWENTY-ONE

The view from the lighthouse was astonishing. The Pacific Ocean and the Tasman Sea colliding – one blue, one green. Honey and Matt sat motionless as they looked at the farthest tip of the North Island. It was a day they would both remember. Honey couldn't remember ever being so happy in the company of a man. All her life she had avoided forming a serious relationship. Today was different, somehow. Matt was different from any man she had ever known. Especially her father.

It was just flashes, like photos in the mind, that stirred up those awful memories of the past. She was just a child. Daddy's favorite. Memories of lying on a towel on her bed as they rubbed her little body with a soapy flannel. Tubes, rubber tubes, water. The memories came in bits and pieces. Nothing tangible, nothing she could grab hold of in her mind and understand. Secrets. Shame. She didn't ask to be Daddy's favorite. She wished she could just play outside like her older sisters did.

She remembered her father waking her on her tenth birthday. "You are a decade old, my little Tinkerbell. Now you are a big girl." Little did she know the secret fondlings under her skirt would evolve into acts that made her cheeks burn and leave red blood spots on her pretty dresses.

It wasn't until that fateful afternoon that everything changed. She remembered wearing her favorite dress. It had belonged to one of her sisters. All her clothes were hand-me-downs – but she didn't care. She had felt so pretty that day. Daddy had said he had a special surprise for her. He had whispered to her when he tucked her in the night before that he would come home early today. He said for her to wait for him in his room after school. Daddy had his own room. He read the bible in his room. No-one was allowed in his room. Except for that day. She remembered waiting for him in her pretty dress wondering what the present could be. Maybe a new bike? She had never had a new bike. Or a dressing table like the girls in the movies had, with a round mirror and flowers painted on the drawers?

It seemed like forever before she heard his footsteps in the hallway. She knew they were all alone. Her sisters often stayed late after school. Ben and Simone didn't live at home anymore. She missed them, especially Ben. She looked up when her father entered the room.

"My little Tinkerbell," he said. Honey liked being called his Tinkerbell. He took off his jacket and hung it in his wardrobe. He kicked off his shoes and began to remove his trousers. Honey looked the other way. She didn't like to see her father getting undressed.

"May I see my present now?" she asked hopefully.

"Not yet, my little Tinkerbell," he said as he folded his trousers on the bed and sat down. Then he patted the space beside him. "Come and sit here and I will show you your present."

It was then that Honey realized that her father didn't have a present for her. She closed her eyes as he inserted her little hand into the opening of his underpants.

Suddenly there was a commotion. Her brother Ben was standing in the room with a look of sheer horror on his face. "You pig! You filthy pig!" How dare you! Your own daughter! Go Honey... Go... Get out of here! Now!"

Honey had fled. She ran across the street to the park and lay on the soft grass and cried. They knew her secret. She was so ashamed. It was all her fault. She liked being Daddy's favorite even though she hated what he did to her.

She stayed at the park for a long time – it was a long time before she heard the sirens coming down the street. When she tried to go back into the house, they stopped her. The police were everywhere.

Simone came and took her to her flat on the other side of town. The next morning her sister said their father and mother were dead. She felt responsible. What had happened? What had Ben done?

When the police asked where she was that day. She told them she was playing in the park across the street. She never told anyone what had happened. No-one. She never would.

Matt took her hand as they walked the track on the high ridge back to their car. "Let's stop at the Mangonui Fish 'n' Chip shop on the way back. I'm hungry. Are you?"

"I'm starving." She shivered in the cold sea breeze.

Matt took off his coat and wrapped it around her shoulders. "I'll keep you warm."

CHAPTER
TWENTY-TWO

Audrey changed her mind and decided to email the death notice to a couple of online newspapers. Short and sweet. She didn't know her uncle very well. She just remembered that when she was a child, he would visit with her father and they would lock themselves in his room and the children were never allowed to intrude. He always smelt the same — of cigarettes and booze. She never trusted the man. Looking back, she wondered what they did all those hours in secret. Maybe it had something to do with those slides her father kept in boxes. She would hear the film projector whirring behind the closed door.

She looked at what she had written.

Stephen John Brown, 73, died Sunday, February 21ˢᵗ, 2016 at the Tiromoana Cabin Resort in Hihi, where he was visiting his family.
He was previously married for twenty-five years to Betty (née Perkins).

Until recently, Mr. Brown lived and worked in Western Australia, driving trucks for numerous Mining Companies. His four nieces, Audrey Wetherby, Becka Simpson, Simone Mayflower and Honey Brown, survive him.

A funeral service will be held tomorrow, 23rd February, at the Kerikeri Funeral Home, followed by a private cremation.

It was done. The funeral was tomorrow. They would all be there. Her sisters had planned to stay until the end of the week. She presumed Matt would stay on too. He and Honey were like two lovebirds. She was happy for Honey – she'd often wondered why Honey had never married. Audrey knew she had suffered more than they had as a child. Her father's debauchery worsened with age. Simone and Becka were less affected by his warped sexual practices. Audrey simply funneled her repulsion into a hatred of all men sharing the same characteristics. Ben was another story. When he discovered what his father had become, he reacted violently. Discovering his mother knew all along of her husband's sexual deviancy made him hate her even more.

Audrey had been there that afternoon. She had walked in on Ben and her father fighting like wild dogs.

She watched silently from the doorway as Ben tried desperately to hold her father down. She feared Ben would lose the battle and her father would kill him. She walked calmly into the kitchen and opened the knife and fork drawer. She was never allowed to touch the carving knife. The knife her father sharpened every Sunday before carving the roast lamb. She would watch him scrape the knife either side of the sharpening tool in a rhythmic and deliberate motion. She removed the big knife and returned to the bedroom. Her father was straddled on top of Ben with his hands tightly around his neck. It was as though she was watching someone else, another girl, stabbing and stabbing, over and over again. The knife was sharp and it cut easily through the plaid shirt and white cotton underpants.

It seemed like a long time before Ben took the knife from her hand. They walked out of the room together and closed the door behind them. Ben knew what to do. He told her to change out of her blood–soaked clothes and run a hot bath. He would take care of everything. She obeyed. Her hand hurt where she had cut it on the knife. She soaked in the bath tilting her head back into the hot water. She was never allowed to bath alone and never with clean water. She was always the second or third one in the bath water and always had to bath with one of her sisters. She had filled the tub right up to the top. Her father couldn't scold her now. She could use all the water she wanted.

Her mind went back to a conversation she had with her father on her fifteenth birthday. He told her she was old enough to support herself and it was time for her to leave home. She didn't care. She couldn't wait to leave. Now she didn't know what would happen. Her father was dead.

Audrey didn't know how long she had stayed in the water, but she did know it was no longer hot when she climbed out and went in search of her brother.

Ben had told her to go for a ride on her bike and not to come back until after the police had come. She never asked Ben why he killed their mother. He just said, "she knew." Audrey had read the diary in her box. The box Ben had kept. Pages and pages of her witnessing the sexual abuse. She had known. For years she had known but had done nothing about it. Ben must have kept the diary to justify what he had done.

The police never knew that Ben and Audrey had been at home that day. They may have suspected it, but proving it was another matter. It was bad enough listening to everyone saying her parents had been such good Christians. Christians, my arse. They were incestuous pedophiles – both of them. If the police knew their parents had been molesting them, they would have had even more reason to suspect them. So they never knew. No-one did. Except, of course, the four sisters and Ben.

CHAPTER
TWENTY-THREE

He held the large carving knife in gloved hands. The knife had been found in the kitchen drawer and had been identified as matching the size and shape of the wounds found on the father's body. It was in the evidence box, marked as 'Exhibit 12'. It had been carefully sealed in a paper bag. The tag said there was no evidence of fingerprints or blood, nothing. But times and forensic science had changed. The detective sent the knife off to the forensics lab – maybe there was some DNA on it. Maybe he would get lucky.

He studied the crime scene photos for the hundredth time. Then he saw them. Three children's school bags in the hallway. He read the report again. The children were not in the house at the time of the murders so why would their school bags be in the house. Had they come home? Had they witnessed the murder? Three school bags? Becka, Audrey and Honey were the only children living in the house and attending school at the time. Were all three involved? Shit! This was big!

"Excuse me?" Higgins looked up and saw a middle-aged woman standing at the counter.

"Can I help you?"

"Are you Detective Constable Higgins? I was told you are handling the Greta Baywater case." The woman leaned towards him urgently.

"There is no case. Greta Baywater died of natural causes."

"She did nothing of the kind." The woman reached into her bag and removed an envelope. "Look at this, then tell me she died of natural causes."

The detective took a familiar pink envelope and removed a handwritten note:

My spirit guides have insisted I contact you.
Your future is in jeopardy.
The love you are seeking is within reach but is hindered by your lack of faith.
I can work on this for you but I will need four sacred candles immediately.
Love and Money will be yours very soon.
Please send me $2,000 to purchase these candles.
Failure to pay the spirit guides can only lead to misfortune.

"When I didn't pay her the $2,000 she sent me another note." The woman handed him another pink envelope containing a note in the same handwriting.

Your lack of faith has resulted in negative energy from my spirit guides.
Your love has turned away and is seeking solace with another woman.
A bad situation is developing at your workplace.
Your job is now in jeopardy.
Eight candles need to be flaming within 48 hours.

Deposit $4,000 immediately as instructed.

Now the woman was distraught. "I didn't have $4,000. I couldn't sleep. Greta was hounding me for the money. Then she died. I got to thinking that if she was asking me for money, maybe she was asking for money from other people from my church. We would all go to her with our problems. No-one spoke about it, but we all knew. I think someone murdered her. It has been on my conscience. Now you know. I have done my duty."

"May I keep these letters?" The detective remembered receiving a call from a crazy woman a few days ago. "I don't suppose you called me before about Greta being a psychic?" he asked.

"No. I didn't. It must have been someone else. She had many, many clients. She did readings for most of the congregation at our church. I don't want the letters. You can keep them. They give me the creeps."

"Your name?" he asked.

"Mary Hastings. I live on the same street at Greta. You can find me in the phone book."

"Thanks, I will be in touch if I need you." The detective watched her leave and immediately compared the handwriting with the handwriting in the letter Greta sent to her nephew before she died. The writing was identical. Who would have guessed? The old lady really was a fortune teller. Or, more likely, a scammer living off other people's fears. I wonder if her nephew knew what she was up to.

He put the letters away in a file. He had bigger fish to fry. He checked the time. *I'm late.* He would have a few words with Audrey Wetherby while he was in Tiromoana. He wondered if

Greta's nephew knew about his aunt's psychic abilities. She must have kept records of her client's readings. Had Ben been one of her clients? He hoped Matt had not destroyed any of her personal effects.

CHAPTER
TWENTY-FOUR

B ecka didn't want to attend her uncle's funeral. It bought back too many memories of the past. He was an awful man. A drunk and a child molester like her father. She had watched Piper yesterday with Simone and John. She admired Simone's choice of lifestyle. They were a happy family and it showed in Piper's attitude to life. She wished her family had stayed whole. She knew it was what happened the afternoon of her parents' deaths that changed the course of her future forever.

That dreadful afternoon she had come home after school to find her brother burning clothes in the incinerator in the kitchen.

"What the heck are you doing?" she had asked him as he squeezed more clothes into the small opening with the poker.

Her brother turned and looked at her. His face was distorted, as if he was in pain. "Go away Becka, this has nothing to do with you."

"I'm not going anywhere," she had insisted. "Tell me what you are doing."

"They're dead. Father and Mother are both dead. He was molesting little Honey. I saw him." He poked at the fire.

She remembered that moment like it was yesterday. "He did it to me too," she whispered.

"I know, and to Audrey. He was an evil man. All that praying, all that preaching about purity and God's will to be chaste and he was molesting his own daughters." Her brother stuffed the rest of the clothes into the incinerator and slammed the door closed.

"Where are they?" she asked.

"He is in his bedroom. Mother is in the lounge.

She knew, you know. She knew everything. She never stopped him. I told her once and she denied it. Told me I was a liar."

Becka turned and headed down the hall to her father's bedroom. She opened the door and gasped. There was blood everywhere. On the walls, on the floor, on the bed, on the rug, everywhere. She looked around the room. She was careful not to stand in the blood. She closed the door and went to find her mother.

Her mother's body lay on the carpet. There was no blood. As she leaned over her she heard her mother gasp. *She is still alive!* Becka remembered the time she told her mother what her father was doing to her. Her mother called her a little slut for saying such things. She took a cushion off the couch and placed it over her mother's face. She held it there for a long time.

Walking back into the kitchen she saw the bloody knife on the kitchen sink. She scrubbed the knife until she was sure all the blood was gone. They waited until the clothes had turned to ashes and the fire had burned itself out. They worked in silence. There were no words to describe how they felt. Not relief or regret. It was just something they knew they had to do.

As they closed the front door and left the house, they understood their lives would never be the same again. They made a pact never to mention what happened that afternoon, and she never did.

CHAPTER
TWENTY-FIVE

A udrey looked up from her desk and into the face of Detective Constable Higgins. "I didn't hear your car," she said.

"I have been here for a while. Been talking to Matt Walters. He said you packed up his aunt's belongings. Did you find any notebooks or diaries by any chance? Mr. Walters said he didn't find any, but I wondered if they might have got mixed up in your brother's things."

"Notebooks? No, can't say I saw anything like that. She did have a number of bibles and odd books. But I don't remember seeing any diary. Why? Do you think she was keeping secrets?" She smiled. "She was just an old religious lady who liked cross-word puzzles. I don't think she had any secrets."

"Everyone has secrets," the detective said. "If you happen to find anything, please let me know. I presume you packed up the house? I see it is on the market."

"He owed more money than the house is worth. The bank is foreclosing on it. I have donated his belongings to the Salvation Army in Whangarei. Mostly old furniture and bits and pieces. You may want to contact them."

"I'll take your word for it. By the way, your parents' murder case is being re-opened. We have found new evidence. I thought you should know."

Fuck! What can he have found? "That is a surprise, detective. The case was closed over thirty years ago. What new evidence could you have possibly found that would warrant re-opening it?"

"I'm sorry but I cannot divulge that information.

Let's just say that we are closer than ever before to solving the case. But you and your sisters will be the first to know when we have something to report."

He's bluffing. What could he possibly have found? "Well, that is good news, detective. Finally my dear parents will be able to rest in peace. My sisters and I have always wondered who was responsible for their deaths. We even suspected our Uncle Steve. He was always fighting with my father. Always coming around for money to buy his booze. But I guess we will never know, now that he is dead," she added.

"Talking about your sisters. You were not at home the afternoon your parents were murdered? Is that right? Your statements suggest you didn't return home from school until after your parents' bodies had been found."

"I have blocked out that awful day. My sisters and I never discuss it. In fact, we have never talked about it to anyone. We all have our own way of dealing with it. But to answer your question, I didn't come home until the police were there. I can't speak for my sisters. But I do know that Honey was at the park that afternoon and Becka was at basketball practice at school. I don't know what time they returned to the house. Our older sister, Simone took us all to her place that night. We didn't go to school the next day."

"I see. That is what I thought. I'm sorry to bring all this up again. But with this new evidence we might want to question you all again. Are your sisters going to be staying here a while?"

"They are due to leave in a couple of days. But I can't imagine what you need to talk to them about. We knew nothing of the murders. We were just children at the time. We have put all that behind us." Audrey knew the detective was onto something. *But what?* "I have to get back to work, detective. Is there anything else?"

"No, not at the moment. I will arrange a time to talk to you all in a couple of days. I would like you all to come to the station. I can send a car for you."

"We are planning on taking a short trip after the funeral. A family road trip down the island. Then Becka is flying back to London on Friday night and Simone and her family are returning home on Saturday morning. If you need to ask any questions I suggest you do so while you are here. We are leaving for Uncle Steve's funeral soon so it will have to be now. I can call them and tell them you want to talk to them. Shall I have them meet you at the picnic table on the front lawn?"

"Yes, but I want to talk to each of them separately."

"I will tell them." She picked up the phone.

CHAPTER
TWENTY-SIX

Simone kept her eyes out to sea. She couldn't look at the detective. He was talking about the afternoon her parents died. She wasn't there when it happened. It was a neighbor who called telling her that the police were at her parents' house and that she should come over.

It had been chaos. Honey ran to her. She was sobbing inconsolably. Becka was sitting on the curve on the footpath with her head in her hands. Audrey was on the front lawn next to her bike. She was in shock. Simone remembered everything so clearly. Her brother wasn't there. He was at work, they said, making deliveries.

She had put her sisters in her car and taken them back to her flat. The police said they wanted to talk to them. She said they would have to wait until tomorrow. She remembered the police asking her who had keys to the house. She had told them they never locked the house. No-one did. It was a safe neighborhood. At least it used to be.

"When did you arrive at the house that afternoon?" the detective asked her now.

"A neighbor called me and told me the police were at the house. I drove straight over there."

"What time was that?"

"It was dinner time. I remember because I had to turn off the vegetables on the stove."

"Were all your sisters there when you arrived?"

"Yes the sirens must have alerted them. They told me that they saw the police at the house when they arrived."

"Was it usual for your sisters to come home late from school?"

"It was not unusual. Becka had basketball practice most afternoons, Audrey liked to stay late and hang out with her friends in the playgrounds. Honey often went to the park after school. As long as they were home by teatime."

"Audrey told me that you don't discuss your parents' murders with each other. Is that right?"

"Yes, we have never talked about it. I know that sounds strange. But we all separated shortly after their murders. Becka went to London; I took a teacher's job in Wellington and married soon after. Honey lived with me for a few years and later moved to Auckland. Audrey traveled overseas. This is the first time we have seen each other in decades. We were not a close family."

"Thanks Simone. Can you ask Becka to join me?"

"I'm sorry detective. But we have to leave for the funeral. They cannot tell you any more than I can. Please leave us alone. Dredging up old memories is too painful. I don't want my younger sisters to go through all that again."

Simone left the detective sitting alone on the picnic bench. He watched as they walked towards the waiting cars. He was surprised to see Matt and Honey hand in hand. *When did that happen?* His gut told him the sisters knew a lot more about their parents' deaths than their original statements indicated. But proving it was another thing.

Three school bags in the hallway on the afternoon of the murder. Three school-age sisters who swore they were not in the house that afternoon. But what reason would they have for murdering their parents? There was no life insurance. The house was heavily mortgaged. Their parents were church-going, respectable people. *I am missing something.*

CHAPTER
TWENTY-SEVEN

I t was over. Uncle Steve was cremated. Well, at least, he would be. They all watched his coffin disappear behind a curtain after the funeral service. It could take up to seventy-two hours to turn her uncle's body into ashes. There were no tears. Simone offered to say a few words. Mostly for Piper's sake. She wanted her daughter to experience the dying process in a respectful manner. Audrey was pleased. She had nothing to say.

On their return, Audrey confessed, "The detective wanted us to come down to the Whangarei police station in a couple of days, but I told him we were planning on taking a road trip immediately after the funeral and wouldn't be able to."

"Good thinking," said Becka. "I don't want to talk to him. Thank goodness I am leaving soon. Hopefully he doesn't bug us again."

"Isn't it against the law to lie to the police?" asked Piper.

"We can just say we changed our minds," Audrey replied.

Arriving back at Tiromoana, Audrey poured herself a full glass of wine and sat in the sun to read her mother's diary. She had read it once before, a long time ago and knew what the words would tell. Opening the old yellowed book at a random page she started reading:

> *Today, he asked me to purchase more film for his camera.*
> *Why does he have to take so many photos? The girls hate being photographed. They cry and try to cover their little bodies because of the shame...*

She couldn't read any more and snapped the book shut. Audrey didn't need confirmation of her parents' sordid lives. After all, she had experienced it at first hand.

Audrey returned the diary to the keepsake box. It was a beautiful carved wooden box her mother had purchased a lifetime ago. A box for her sordid secrets. She touched her mother's pearls. Audrey had worn them home the day her brother died but had not worn them since. *Such a beautiful necklace.* Why her brother had the pearls she would never know. She placed the pearls under the diary and closed the lid.

Becka, Honey and Matt arrived for pre-dinner drinks on the lawn. Audrey was surprised to find she actually liked having her sisters around. Somehow meeting again as adults allowed them to disconnect themselves from their childhood.

"To family and friends," she toasted. "I am going to miss you when you go."

"Family and friends," they chorused.

CHAPTER
TWENTY-EIGHT

He looked at the crime scene photos again. Something else was bugging him. What was it? He searched through the evidence box and every crime scene photo but nothing seemed to ring a bell.

Detective Constable Higgins walked over to his collage on the wall. He had added headshots to every name. Then he realized what it was. Mrs. Brown was wearing the same twinset in the newspaper article as on the day she was killed. The only difference was – she was not wearing the pearls. There was no mention of the pearls in the report. He searched the evidence documents. No pearls. He knew he had seen them somewhere, but where?

He prided himself on his eidetic memory, which was usually found only in children. He had the ability to recall images, sounds or objects in memory only after a short time of being exposed to them. This made him an excellent detective. He had solved numerous cases by utilizing his special talent. *The answer is always in the details.*

Then, as clear as if he had seen them yesterday, he saw them in his mind's eye around Audrey Wetherby's neck on the first day he met her. He had interviewed her in her brother's library and she was wearing the very same pearls. I wonder when she took ownership of her mother's pearls? Surely her mother would not have given them to a fifteen-year-old girl? She must have taken them after her death. But when? That is the question.

He made a note in his file and spotted a pile of boxes in his office marked "Murray Brown". They must have arrived today from the Christchurch office. He opened the first box and saw stacks of Kodak slide carousels. He pulled a slide out and held it up to the light. A waterfall. Looked like Milford Sound. He looked at a number of slides at random – all scenes mostly from the West Coast of the South Island. He presumed that Mr. Brown must have been an avid amateur photographer. There were undeveloped rolls of film and a camera. He opened up the other boxes. More slides, more film. He closed the boxes and stacked them aside in his office. He requested a projector. When it arrived he would review all the slides. Maybe they held some clues.

CHAPTER
TWENTY-NINE

They sat in rows on straight-backed chairs. Deacon James welcomed them to the meeting. "I'm glad you could all make it," he began. He looked around the room at his fellow Christians. "I called this meeting to discuss the death of Greta Baywater and how she had affected our lives over the past ten years. Many of you have come to me and confessed the shame you have felt when this woman threatened to expose your private conversations with her. I also have experienced her wrath. But we are not here to discuss what she held over us, but rather to put an end to this once and for all.

"I have contacted her nephew, Matt Walters, asking him for assistance in this matter, requesting he destroy any records his aunt kept of our conversations. I am hoping he is an honest man and will agree to our request."

"If he agrees, how will we know whether he has destroyed them?" asked a middle-aged woman from the back row. "What if he uses the same information to destroy us?"

"It is unlikely he will read all her private correspondence. We will just have to take his word. Our goal is to have everything destroyed. Don't you agree? More importantly, we don't want the police knowing our personal business. Do we?"

Mary Hastings was listening in silence. She had already gone to the police and given him the blackmail letters. Should she tell the others? Better to keep quiet. They may not want the police to know.

Deacon James had a lot to hide. His marital infidelity would get him banned from his church. Infidelity with another man would destroy his reputation completely. He had gone to Greta ten years ago. Craig, his lover at the time, had recommended her. It will be completely confidential, he was promised. Confidential, my ass. She had used his sessions to blackmail him ever since. At first his sessions with Greta were therapeutic. She made him feel good about himself. Every Wednesday, week after week, he would sit in the little library and she would bring out her tarot cards. "Your future looks bright. Your secret is safe," she would say. He had confessed that his marriage to the beautiful daughter of the wealthiest family in the community was a farce. He was attracted to men. Then, a few months ago, Greta had threatened him. Wanted money. Lots of money. Now she was dead. Did she keep records of their sessions? He presumed she did, and they must be destroyed.

He looked at the crowd in the room. He was shocked at how many had responded to the notice in last week's church bulletin:

If you have had a reading with Greta Baywater and suffered consequences please attend a meeting in the Church Hall on Tuesday night at 7 p.m.

He recalled most of them had also attended her funeral. He

wondered if they felt relief, like he did, when they realized she could no longer destroy their lives. Did they also worry that their meetings had been recorded or, worse, documented for anyone to see?

He hoped that Matt Walters would acquiesce to his request. He asked the attendees to email him immediately after the meeting so he could respond to them when he heard any news.

The crowd dispersed. Deacon James checked his messages for the tenth time that night. No response. *Damn!*

CHAPTER
THIRTY

att wondered what Deacon James could possibly want that was so urgent. When he read his text message about destroying his aunt's notes pertaining to their private sessions, he thought the man must have lost his mind. What sessions? What notes? What church sessions could possibly stir up so much emotion? He would return his call later. Matt was looking forward to spending the day with Honey. She had stayed over again last night in his cabin. They drank and laughed and told silly stories until they fell asleep. He had never felt so blissfully happy.

Today they would spend the day at Tiromoana, exploring the rocky beaches and fishing for snapper off table rock. It was a beautiful day. Honey had left to help with breakfast and to sneak a couple of bottles of wine for their day in the sun.

"Mr. Walters, Mum sent me over to tell you that brunch is ready on the front lawn," It was Piper.

"Thanks Piper. But you can call me Matt. I'm on my way." He watched the pretty teen in short shorts and bikini top skip down the wooded path. *Youth. So much energy.* He grabbed his camera. His creative juices were flowing. Beautiful women, stunning views and warm balmy breezes. It doesn't get any better than this. His phone started beeping again. *Shit. What is his problem?* He turned off his phone and went to join the others.

CHAPTER
THIRTY-ONE

Deacon James could wait no longer. It had been twelve hours since he left the first message and still he had no reply. Has he read her notes? Is he planning to blackmail us all too? He needed to get answers. His life depended on it. Where was her nephew staying? Researching online didn't reveal anything. Greta's personal life was just that, personal. If she had a website or Facebook page, it was taken down. Nothing.

He prepared himself for the seven o'clock prayer meeting. He expected a large turnout tonight. He knew God would take second place to Greta. They would want to know if he had handled everything like he said he would. He picked up his bible and headed for the door.

His phone rang; he looked at the caller ID. Finally! "Matt Walters here, you left me a message or two. Sorry I haven't returned your call until now but I have been out fishing all day. Just got back. What can I do for you? You said something about my aunt having notes about sessions?"

"It is rather a personal matter, Mr. Walters. Your aunt was

assisting a number of her friends and now that she has passed away, we would prefer to have any information she may have recorded, destroyed."

"I am sorry, Deacon James. I have no idea what you are talking about. My aunt was just a housekeeper and caregiver. You must have her confused with someone else."

"You didn't know?"

"Know what?"

"Your aunt was a psychic. She had quite a reputation – used tarot cards to look into the future. Unfortunately she used private information gained from her sessions to encourage her clients to pay her large sums of money."

"No way, you say my Aunt Greta was a fortune teller?" Matt laughed. "I have her personal effects. Just some old bibles, pieces of cheap jewelry and boxes of clothes. She lived with Ben Brown for over fifteen years, taking care of him. She liked doing crossword puzzles and knitting. I am sorry Deacon James, but I cannot help you. You are mistaken. My aunt was a nice church-going lady."

"I have proof; letters, requests for payment. Blackmail. I am not mistaken. Please look through her belongings again."

Blackmail? The man is nuts. He explained. "Audrey, Ben's sister collected all her belongings and kept them in storage for me. There is nothing here to indicate that my aunt was black-mailing anyone."

"Would you mind if I look through her belongings for myself? I wouldn't ask but you can appreciate this is a very deli-cate situation. I would be most grateful and if there is nothing, as you say, then I can tell the others that the horrible ordeal is over and we can all go back to our lives in peace. It would mean a lot to us," he pleaded.

Matt paused. He knew that he wouldn't hear the last of this

man if he didn't give him what he wanted. "I am staying up here in the far north. The place is called Tiromoana at Hihi. We could meet tomorrow morning at ten. Would that work for you?"

"Thank you. I am most grateful. Ten it is."

As soon as Matt hung up the phone, he regretted his offer. Somehow it didn't seem so far fetched that his aunt might be a psychic and even blackmailing her clients. He had wondered why she was so desperate to leave her employment and home and stay with him. She had sounded afraid. *Afraid she would get caught!*

He almost admired her spunk. Here he thought she was just a boring old lady when in fact she was an entrepreneur, a therapist and a blackmailer. Who knew?

Tonight, after dinner, he would ask Audrey if she knew what his aunt had been up to. Ask her if she knew of any notebooks or records. He doubted she knew any more than he did. But it would make for a colorful conversation. He grinned at the thought.

CHAPTER
THIRTY-TWO

Detective Constable Higgins had been sitting in the same chair for hours. He stood up and stretched. He was on his twelfth carousel of slides. It wasn't that Murray Brown was a bad photographer; in fact, he was quite a good one. It was the quantity, not quality, that had become exhausting. Higgins knew he would never need to travel the west coast of New Zealand ever again. Every scene was firmly imprinted on his mind. Unfortunately forever.

He picked up the thirteenth carousel and took out the first slide. Holy Shit! Higgins couldn't believe what he was looking at. He put it to one side and pulled out the next slide, then the next, and the next. The images on the screen shocked and repulsed him. *Now it all makes sense.* The man was molesting children. His own children. Who would have thought a lay preacher, a pillar of the church was an incestuous pedophile. *Who knew? Did Ben Brown know? Was he molested too?* Higgins turned off the projector. *This was a game changer. New evidence. Now he had something to work with.*

Higgins looked at the crime wall and studied the family

more closely. He always believed Murray and Sophie Brown's murders were personal. Strangulation is certainly up close and personal. Multiple stabbings indicate anger and revenge. Any one of the children may have had cause to attack their parents.

He had a gut feeling that Audrey Wetherby was hiding something. Was a fifteen-year-old girl capable of such vicious crime? Yes, he decided, definitely.

CHAPTER
THIRTY-THREE

Honey and Matt joined Audrey for a late-night drink in the cottage. The others had retired to bed after a day in hot summer sun.

"She was a psychic conning her clients out of large sums of money. Who would have thought? No wonder she was in a hurray to leave," Matt confided. "Did you know what she was up to, Audrey?"

"I had no idea. She was a strange one, I'll give you that." Audrey considered her options. "Now I come to think about it, I did find some books in the library that must have been hers. Books about tarot and witchcraft. I wondered why my brother had taken an interest in such things."

"Do you still have them?"

"I think so. I'll sort through the boxes tomorrow and find them for you."

"Deacon James is particularly interested in any records or notes she may have kept. He is worried. His congregation is worried, and he wants them destroyed."

Honey looked over at Audrey and asked, "I don't suppose Ben was one of her clients?"

Audrey knew exactly why she was worried. "No. I am sure he wasn't." She knew exposing Greta's past would steer any suspicion away from her. "Why was Deacon James so worried? Was he one of her clients too?" she asked.

"It would appear so. I wonder what he has to hide?"

Audrey was curious herself. So much so she bid Honey and Matt goodnight and immediately settled down to read Greta's prolific hand-written records.

First she would find and remove any reference to Ben. She started reading.

Ben can't sleep. He is restless and remorseful. I suggested he have a reading. He was extremely reluctant. He has secrets. Secrets he is not ready to share.

It has taken almost three months to convince Ben a reading would ease his mind. He finally agreed today. I couldn't imagine what was troubling him. The cards don't lie. The ten of swords shows violence in his past. Then he confessed he has done something really bad. He murdered someone. He wouldn't say whom. Just that it has haunted him his whole life.

The cards confirm this.

Audrey searched through her notes and found more entries:

I did another reading for Ben. This time the cards showed two deaths – a man and a woman. I asked him if he knew who they were. He was silent. I won't press him but we don't have much time. The cards show his death is near. I will know when it is time. I found a box belonging to Ben's mother. Why he keeps it near to his bed, I don't know. While he slept I read his mother's diary. She was

a wicked woman. There was much incest in his family. Did Ben kill his mother? His father?
Am I in danger too?

There was one last entry:

Ben is surrounded by death. His death and other deaths. When I look deeper into the meaning of the cards I see my own death is imminent.
I must protect myself. I must leave this place. Too much death. Too much suffering.

Audrey carefully removed all the pages referencing Ben and sat back to read the entire notebook.

Two hours later she had an insight into almost every member of the Baptist Church in Whangarei. The most damaging confessions belonged to Deacon James. Who would have thought the man who was known as the pillar of society was not only unfaithful to his high-society wife but was unfaithful with men. Of course, Audrey was not judgmental, at least not of homosexuality; after all, her greatest love was with a woman. It was his dishonesty – portraying piousness in public and concealing his sexual preference in private – just like her father.

She hadn't had so much fun in ages. Pages and pages of self-righteous Christians with their petty crimes and misdemeanors; extramarital affairs, stealing petty cash from the work till, sexual addiction, food addiction, alcohol addiction, gay tendencies, stalking, coveting their neighbor's wife – it was all there.

There must have been over fifty clients Greta had been blackmailing in some form or another. Either with regular readings costing a hundred dollars each or, worse, a demand for large amounts of cash to purchase special sacred candles. Audrey had never seen any candles in the house so presumed this was just a scam to keep the old women in comfort when it was time to pack up and disappear. Shame she never got to make it out the front door.

Audrey decided to show the notebook to Matt tomorrow. She had no interest in its contents. Matt could decide what he wanted to do with it. Personally she felt Greta's clients had suffered enough. As for Deacon James, the fact that she knew his sordid little secret and now had copies of all his readings with Greta, meant he could cause her no trouble in the future. She returned to her printer and scanned the last few pages, just to be sure. Proof of Greta's criminal past was her protection against any incrimination in the future.

CHAPTER
THIRTY-FOUR

Deacon James drove his BMW along the Hihi waterfront. Beautiful. If he wasn't on such an unfortunate expedition he might choose to stay a while. Get in some fishing. He took the gravel road up the peninsula, admiring the clear blue waters of Doubtless Bay. Taking the first driveway on the left, he headed towards the red-roofed cottage.

She was picking peaches from a tree and turned as he approached. "Beautiful day. You must be Deacon James. Matt said you were stopping by this morning. You will find him on the front lawn with my sister, Honey." She pointed in the direction of the ocean.

As he approached the couple sitting on the lawn he couldn't help but notice the shirtless body of the man sprawled on the grass. He was taut and bronze, making his groin ache with desire. He didn't usually get the gay vibe from heterosexual men and wondered if Matt Walters went both ways.

"Steve James; you must be Matt Walters," he introduced himself.

"Steve, nice to meet you." Matt stood and offered him a deck chair. "Would you like a beer or home-made lemonade?"

"A lemonade would be great, thanks," Deacon James said as he reclined in the chair. "Great view you have here."

"This is Audrey's sister, Honey," Matt said, introducing him to the lovely blonde in a large white hat and huge sunglasses.

"Nice to meet you," he said politely. She smiled.

"So you have come to rummage through my Aunt's belongings? Do you know what you are looking for exactly?" Matt enquired.

"I hope there is nothing to find. Then we will know everyone's readings are free from scrutiny."

Audrey joined them on the lawn. She was carrying a notebook and a fresh jug of lemonade. She poured him a glass and handed him the book. "I think this is what you are looking for."

Deacon James opened the book and within seconds he knew she was right. "Yes, sadly it is." He was quiet as he read page after page in the afternoon sun. Matt and Honey had already skimmed through the book and knew of its contents. Matt was horrified his aunt had used the information to torture the minds of her clients. He was happy to give the notebook to Deacon James.

"We are giving you the notebook," said Audrey, "on the condition you destroy it. It is of no value to you or to any of your congregation. It can only do harm. Matt doesn't want his aunt's name dragged through the courts or social media and I am sure you don't want yours to be either. Can we agree that the book is to be destroyed?"

"Yes," he agreed.

A car pulled into the car park. It was Detective Constable Higgins. As the detective walked towards them, Deacon James quickly concealed the notebook in his trouser pocket.

"Glad I caught you. I thought you were on a trip, Audrey. I am surprised to find you all here."

"We changed our mind and decided to stay here at Tiro-moana. What brings you up this way, detective?" Honey peered up at the detective blocking the sun.

"Just following up on a couple of loose ends," the detective said pointedly.

Bloody Hell! "Would you like a glass of lemonade?" Audrey offered.

"Love one." The detective took a seat at the picnic table. "Beautiful day.

"*It was until you arrived.* "Yes, it is."

CHAPTER
THIRTY-FIVE

D etective Constable Higgins recognized Steve James. He ran with the rich and famous in Whangarei. His wife, Naomi, was an attorney and Higgins had dealt with her on a number of occasions. He wondered what James was doing here at Tiromoana. "Steve James," he said in recognition. "I didn't know you knew Audrey Wetherby."

"We have just met," explained Audrey. "He stopped by to check out the accommodation. He and his wife are thinking of taking a holiday up this way."

"Greta was a member of your church, wasn't she? So you know Greta's nephew, Matt Walters?"

"Yes, we've met. Small world isn't it?" Deacon James stood to leave. "Thanks, Audrey, for your hospitality. I will call you to confirm the dates."

"Nice to meet you. We'll talk soon," Audrey said pointedly. "So detective, what can I do for you?"

Higgins looked at Matt "I don't suppose you had any idea that your aunt was doing psychic readings for members of her church?"

Deacon James kept walking towards his car. Higgins knew he had heard him.

Matt laughed. "I didn't know my aunt very well, detective. What makes you think that?"

"I had a complaint from someone who showed me a number of letters from Greta requesting large sums of money or she would divulge their innermost secrets. I don't suppose you know anything about that?"

"I'm sorry detective. That is very unfortunate. Maybe it explains why she was in such a hurry to leave town," Matt offered.

Higgins looked at Audrey. "Did you know about this? Did your brother know?"

"I had no idea, though I always thought she was a strange old woman." Audrey walked away from the group on the lawn. "Honey, can you give me a hand in the laundry?" she called back.

"Sure, Audrey." Honey followed her sister, leaving Higgins and Matt chatting in the afternoon sun.

"How well do you know Audrey and her sisters?" Higgins asked.

"I know Honey pretty well. We have become quite close over the past few days. She is a wonderful person. Audrey is a different story. She is rather cold and aloof. Always has a smile. But something doesn't add up with her; why do you ask?"

"Thirty years ago their parents were murdered and, to date, no-one has been held responsible for the crime."

"Holy shit! I had no idea. Honey told me the sisters were estranged since their childhood. Now I know why. It must have been traumatic, to say the least. Was anyone suspected of the crime?"

The detective paused. "The children were all questioned at

the time. Their stories were never consistent. The police at the time suspected the brother was responsible. None of the children had a solid alibi. Now new evidence has come to light. We are reopening the case."

"Shit! Poor Honey. Does she know the case is being reopened?"

"I have told Audrey. I presume she has told her sisters."

"Don't bet on it. What is the new evidence? Do you have a suspect?"

"It turns out their father was an avid photographer. Thousands of slides have been located in the cold case files shedding new light on the case." The detective knew he had said enough. Matt Walters would pass on the information to the women. That was what Higgins had come here for. He knew the women would not talk to him. Now they might have second thoughts, especially if they knew their secret was exposed. He would wait for one of them to contact him.

"Well, I just stopped by to talk to you about your aunt. Messy stuff. Hope her death has put an end to it all. I'd keep your distance from Deacon James. I never liked that guy. He's hiding something. I wouldn't want to get on his bad side."

The detective waved goodbye to the women as he departed. They didn't wave back.

CHAPTER
THIRTY-SIX

Becka was horrified. "They found *what*?"

"He said thousands of slides. Said your father was a photographer. Did you know?"

"We knew." Simone looked at her glass of wine, avoiding her sisters' glares. "We knew he took photos. He and Uncle Steve would spend hours in his room looking at them."

"Why would the police be interested in the slides? Do you suppose they were of other women?" Matt looked at Honey.

"I don't want to talk about it," said Honey. "I'm going to bed. I'm tired. I'll see you all in the morning."

"I'll come with you," said Matt, walking with her to the door.

"I want to be alone tonight," Honey said. "You stay here and finish your wine. I'll see you tomorrow before I head off home. It's time to rescue my cats and get back to work. Goodnight."

Matt looked upset. *I blew it! Fuck the detective. I shouldn't have said anything.* "I'm off to bed too."

Simone, Becka and Audrey watched Matt leave and knew that they must finally talk about that afternoon.

The detective had obviously seen for himself their father's sexual deviancy. Their secret was out.

"What are we going to do?" Simone was the first to talk.

"What can we do?" Becka knew she would never confess her crime to her sisters. "We weren't there. Surely he doesn't suspect that we had anything to do with it?"

"Maybe he has found some DNA. They didn't have DNA technology then. Maybe they know who did it." Simone was hopeful.

"DNA on what? Our DNA would be everywhere, we lived in the house, for heaven's sake." Audrey thought about the knife. *Do they have the knife? She knew it was time. Time to tell.* "He did it. Ben killed them. I came home that afternoon and found Father on the floor. There was blood everywhere. Ben told me to leave and not come back until the police arrived. It was awful!" She lowered her head. Everyone would believe her. Ben was dead. No-one would ever find out the truth.

"I know," said Becka. I was there too.

Audrey's mind froze. She was there? When?

Becka continued, "Father was already dead. I helped Ben get rid of the evidence. At least I thought I did.

I washed the knife and helped him burn the bloody clothes."

"You never said anything; why not?" Simone had turned pale and looked at her two sisters in shock. "Why didn't you tell me?"

"What about Mother? Was she dead too?" Audrey asked.

"Yes. Her body was lying on the lounge floor. Both were dead. Ben said not to say anything. They deserved it. He would have gone to jail if anyone knew. I promised him." Becka turned away.

"So Ben killed them both?" Simone was beginning to realize the seriousness of what she just heard. Do you think the detective knows?"

"No. How could he? Why re-open the case now?" Becka was obviously upset.

"If he has seen the photos, he knows we were all abused. He may think we all had something to do with their murders." Simone offered as an explanation.

Audrey knew she had Ben's written confession torn from Greta's notebook. He had confessed to their mother's murder. He had not confessed to their father's. She knew that would be a problem. "We do not have to talk to the police. We have the right to remain silent, no matter what. If the detective questions us, we can ask for an attorney. Unless he can prove we had something to do with their murders we cannot be implicated."

"Won't he think we have something to hide if we ask for an attorney?" Simone asked. "Personally, I think we should just say that we had nothing to do with it."

"If he insists on questioning us, I agree. But if he brings us to the station for questioning, I agree with Audrey. We should ask for an attorney. Who knows what evidence they have. Maybe we will all be locked up." Becka knew she was to blame for her mother's death. What if they knew? But how could they?

"I always suspected Ben killed them," Simone confessed. "The night they died, the police took him down to the station and questioned him for hours. He came back to my place afterwards and looked devastated. You were all asleep. I asked him if he had done it. He said he was working, making deliveries. Hadn't even been there. I wanted to believe him. The police wouldn't leave it alone. They hounded me. Audrey, you remember? They questioned you for hours, too."

"I wasn't there," Audrey lied. "I arrived home after the police turned up. But you were there, Becka? You helped Ben clean away the evidence? You must have left before the police arrived."

"I told the police I knew nothing. I think they suspected Ben. Only because he was the oldest. They couldn't prove anything. If the police have seen the photos, they may think we all had a motive. I leave for London in a couple of days. Hopefully I can avoid talking to them before I go."

"I think we should head home tomorrow. We need to get Piper back to school anyway. Don't communicate by phone or email in case the police have us bugged. Tell Honey not to talk about it either. Hopefully Matt will let the subject drop. I don't think Honey can cope with a relationship *and* the past being dredged up. Poor Honey. She suffered the most. Didn't she? Daddy's little girl, what bullshit!"

"They deserved what they got. I don't blame Ben for doing what he did," said Becka.

Audrey poured another glass of wine as her sisters bade goodnight. Fuck the detective. Why couldn't he leave it alone?

CHAPTER
THIRTY-SEVEN

M att couldn't sleep. An online search had revealed the whole gruesome story. Newspaper articles from thirty years ago gave all the details. He looked at the photo of Honey's parents on the front page of *The Christchurch Press*. He read how the police suspected Ben. *I wonder if Greta knew? I hope she wasn't blackmailing him, too.* Now he knew why Audrey had kept Greta's notebook. He knew it couldn't have got mixed up with Ben's stuff. Audrey must have suspected she knew. Did she remove any evidence? Did Ben confess before dying? Was Greta afraid of Ben? Maybe her death wasn't a result of natural causes.

Why would the detective mention Honey's father's photos? He obviously wanted him to tell the women. But why? What were the photos of? Why were the girls so upset when he mentioned them? His mind was spinning. He looked over at Honey's cabin and saw that her light was still on. It was after midnight. He missed sleeping with her. She was so soft and warm. He missed the smell and feel of the woman. He grabbed a bottle of wine from his fridge and headed over to her.

It was obvious she had been crying. He took her in his arms and she sobbed on his shoulder. They were standing in the doorway. He wiped away her tears and took her hand. "Come, let's talk," he said, steering her towards the sofa in the corner of the cabin.

"Was it the photos that upset you?" Matt asked.

She nodded.

"What are in the photos that upset you so much?"

"I can't say."

"Is it something to do with your parents' deaths?"

She nodded.

"Do you know who killed them?" he asked

"Please don't ask me. I can't talk about it." She blew her nose and wiped her eyes.

"You don't have to say anything. I am here for you. Would you like me to stay here tonight so you are not alone?"

She nodded.

He held her until the sun rose. She tossed and turned throughout the night. He knew it was bad, whatever it was. His poor Honey. What had they done to her?

CHAPTER
THIRTY-EIGHT

Detective Constable Higgins knew he should bring in the Brown sisters and confront them with the new evidence to see if they would talk. He had their father's incestuous photos and the crime scene photo of their schoolbags in the hallway proving they were in the house before or during the murder. Although being victims of child molestation and incest didn't make them murderers, the presence of their schoolbags in the hallway needed to be explained. Did they witness their brother killing their parents? Did they participate in the killings?

He had not wanted to discuss it yesterday at Audrey's. Matt Walters was there and he was surprised to see Deacon James there too. Something fishy going on, he was sure of it. He would prefer to have Audrey and her sisters come into the station where their interview could be recorded and documented officially.

He needed to act quickly before Becka flew back to England. Audrey had said she was leaving soon. He needed to bring them in to the station today. He picked up the phone and called Audrey.

"I'm sorry detective. You have missed them all.

They left first thing this morning."

"Has Becka left for London?"

"Her flight is tonight. She is driving down to Auckland. She'll be back in England in forty-eight hours. If you wanted to talk to us why didn't you do so yesterday when you were here?"

"I prefer to hold the interviews at the station," he replied.

"Interviews? Now it is an interview? We have nothing to say, detective. Nothing that we didn't say thirty years ago."

"I think you might want to see what new evidence we have uncovered."

"Does this evidence implicate any of us?" she asked.

"Well, actually it does involve you, Honey and Becka," he replied.

"Can't you just tell me what it is?" Audrey's voice didn't waiver, but her heart was beating loudly in her chest.

"It is proof that all three of you were in the house when the murders took place."

Fuck! What the hell! "You must be mistaken. We did not go into the house at all that afternoon. The police wouldn't let us in. We stayed at Simone's that night. I can't imagine what evidence you think you have?"

"I can't divulge that over the phone. You need to come into the station. Could you make it this afternoon?"

"I'm sorry detective, that is impossible. I have to prepare all the cabins for guests who are arriving later today. I have nothing to say to you. If you keep insisting I will have to get an attorney. Please do not harass me anymore. Good day, detective." She hung up. *Fuck him. He is bluffing.*

Well. So Audrey is threatening to lawyer up. Why, I wonder? What does she have to hide? He only had circumstantial evidence. Nothing that would enable him to obtain a warrant for her arrest. He needed help. Someone on the inside. And he knew exactly who that could be.

CHAPTER
THIRTY-NINE

udrey couldn't warn her sisters. They had agreed not to communicate, at least not until all of it had died down. She wished she could tell them the detective was on a mission. He would track them down, she was sure of it. She did have a code she could text them. She sent it: *Hope you got home safely.* Anodyne to anyone else but a warning they should be careful. She hoped it would be enough.

All six cabins were fully booked tonight. Her sisters had helped her prepare their cabins before they left. She just had to provide fresh linen, flowers, and wine and write the "welcome" notes. Audrey took pride in her business. Her website was overflowing with guests' favorable comments. "Loved our stay at Tiromoana"; "Our cabin was divine"; "Audrey is a wonderful host"; "Highly recommend Tiromoana Cabin Resort – the best accommodation in Northland."

Guests began arriving in the late afternoon. Honeymoon couples, fishermen, a wonderful elderly couple, and a family of four. It was almost eight o'clock before Audrey could settle down to a movie and a glass of wine. She breathed a sigh of relief. Always preferring a solitary lifestyle, she found it exhausting to welcome and entertain guests and play hostess. Tonight she had some much-needed alone time. Tomorrow a few of the guests were checking out. It would be another busy day.

CHAPTER
FORTY

Eric Chapman was surprised to get the call. He hadn't heard from Higgins since he had turned private eye. They used to work together. Higgins got promoted to Detective. Chapman preferred the freedom of being self-employed. They both had gone their separate ways.

"Higgins. Bloody Higgins. What can I do you for? Long time no hear."

He was pleased to get a job. It had been a while. Higgins gave him a complete run-down of what the job entailed. Surveillance and reporting. All expenses paid and a healthy commission upon results.

He made the reservation and headed up north, radio blaring, windows down and a couple of dozen beer in the back seat. Life was good!

The Hihi Motor Camp was busy. He had reserved one of the furnished motel units on site. The camp was across the road from Hihi beach. Grabbing a beer and ignoring the "no alcohol" sign on the beach, he sat on the sand and watched the setting sun. Tomorrow he would start clocking the hours.

Tonight he would take a trip into Mangonui and grab some fish and chips and a beer.

He looked up the gravel road towards the peninsula. He was told it was only about a mile walk along the road. When the tide was out, he could walk along the rocky beach. Either way he would need to be discreet. Maybe take a fishing rod and gear. He could catch a snapper while he was at it.

CHAPTER
FORTY-ONE

Becka had not moved from the old wooden bench for over an hour. Whenever life became unbearable, she found peace in her childhood memories of the Christchurch Botanical Gardens. The familiar curved bridge leading into the gardens from the car park overlooked the Avon River where Becka sat watching the ducks bobbing in and out of the clear water. She wished she had bread to throw into the water as they did when they were children.

She had such few happy childhood memories. She would daydream that one day her "real" family would knock at their door and explain she had been mistakenly given to the wrong mother at birth. But that never happened. Instead, she had murdered her mother and – as soon as she could after that – she had left for London.

She felt in her pocket for her return ticket to London. She hadn't told her sisters about her plan to visit their hometown. They presumed that she had flown from Auckland to Heathrow. It was better they never knew. It was time to revisit the past.

She parked across the road from the familiar quaint old bungalow. It hadn't changed over the years.

She was seventeen years old when she had fallen in love with David. He was a senior at high school and one year older than she was. If Ben had not gone crazy that night, she would most likely have married David. But after her parents were murdered and the constant publicity had turned their lives into a nightmare, David didn't want anything to do with her. She had gone to see him the next day and he wouldn't even look at her. Then he stopped talking to her altogether. He had broken her heart.

Someone was in the kitchen. A woman. She waited. A car pulled into the driveway and a middle-aged man with a big belly and baggy sweats appeared carrying an old gym bag. She took her chance. "David? David Knowles?"

It was with complete disinterest that he turned towards her. "It's Becka Brown," she said. "Long time no see."

"Well fuck me! I thought you were living in England!"

"I was. I am," she said. "You may have heard, my brother, Ben, died recently and I came for the funeral."

"Yeah. Read it in the paper."

"So you are married?" she asked, looking towards the house.

"Yes. I think you knew her. Mary Morris. You were in the same class?"

"I didn't know you even knew Mary," she said, surprised. "She was one of my best friends."

"Oh, was she? She didn't tell me that. In fact, she said that you were not close at all." He looked at her with spiteful contempt. "What can I do for you, Becka?"

"I was in the old neighborhood and wondered if you still lived in the old house."

"Yes, my parents passed away not long ago and Mary and I

moved into the house. I always loved this old house." He ran his hand over his thinning hair and turned as his wife appeared on the front porch.

"Mary, come here. It's Becka Brown. Remember, from high school."

"Of course, I remember Becka," she said smugly.

"You had the hots for my David. Sad thing about your parents being murdered. Did they ever find out who did it?"

Becka ignored the question. "Well must be off. Have heaps to do before I head back to London."

As she returned to the car she watched the couple walk inside and shut the front door.

It wasn't until almost midnight when the fire brigade was called to 311 Pine Avenue. The old wooden heritage home was burned to the ground. Two bodies were discovered in the ashes. No-one knew how the fire started. Only the family cat had escaped.

CHAPTER
FORTY-TWO

She didn't mean to stare. The man fishing off the rock, her rock, was beautiful. He was perfect in every way. Audrey didn't like fat men, short men or men with big heads. They were repulsive to her. This man, whoever he was, was tall, lean and muscular. He was completely oblivious to her presence. The gravel road from Tiromoana to the water's edge was hidden from the shore. She had chosen to take a walk rather than drive her Rav4 to the beach. She stood at the opening between the pohutakawa trees, admiring the stranger on her shore.

Audrey was pleased she was wearing her favorite summer dress and yellow sandals. Her skin was bronzed from the summer months. A wide floppy hat and sunglasses were her usual accessories achieving both anonymity and protection from the blistering sun. She knew she looked good. She sat on the grassy slope careful not to soil her pale-yellowdress. Wrapping her arms around her knees she waited patiently for the gorgeous man to turn in her direction.

"Oh!" he exclaimed. "I didn't see you there. Where did you come from?" He began winding in his line.

Audrey apologized. "I didn't mean to disturb you. Catch anything?"

"Nope. Not a thing. But I can't complain. It's such a beautiful spot." He grabbed his tackle box and climbed down the rock towards her.

"Are you from around here?" Audrey presumed he was either staying in one of the holiday homes or at the motor camp. He was too clean cut for a local guy.

"From Auckland. Came up for some fishing and to get out of the city for a few days. You?"

"I'm a local." He was standing so close to her she could smell him. A mixture of sea air and musk. It had been a while since she had been with a man. Audrey hadn't known she was bi until her relationship with a woman a year ago. It didn't end well.

"You are not dressed for fishing or walking on the rocks," he said looking at her ridiculously strappy sandals. "How did you get here?"

Audrey laughed. "You are right. I came down the road behind me."

"There is a road?" He sounded shocked. "I thought the only way to the fishing spot is by walking half a mile along the rocks. Now you tell me there's a road?"

"Well it's not a public road. It's private property.

But I know the owner." She smiled as he sat down beside her and stretched his long legs down the bank.

As they talked the tide came in and the water began to lap at their feet. "You won't be able to return back to the main beach now the tide is in," Audrey said. "I guess you will have to trespass on private property and take the road back."

"Are you sure the owner won't mind?"

"No. If you stick with me you will be fine." He offered his hand as they climbed up the bank to the gravel road. She wished she had worn more sensible shoes for climbing the steep incline. As they reached the top of the road she opened the gate and together they walked along the long grassy ridge, past the cabins, to the gated entranceway on the far side. "I didn't know this place existed," the man said. "Looks like a nice place to stay."

"It is," she said as they reached the driveway to the main road. "I'm sorry, it is quite a walk down the road to the Hihi beach but it is a lot easier than walking along the rocks."

"Thanks," he said. "Appreciate it." He threw his rod over his shoulder and, with tackle box in hand, headed off towards the Hihi township below.

He'd left and hadn't even asked her name. She was disappointed. There again, she hadn't asked for his. Two strangers on a rocky beach on a sunny afternoon. He obviously wasn't attracted to her. *Damn. He was gorgeous.*

Audrey turned on the six o'clock news. The lead story was about a fire in Christchurch. Two bodies discovered.

"The names have just been released of the two bodies found following a fire at 311 Pine Avenue in Papanui, Christchurch. They were David and Mary Knowles, a married couple who had recently moved into their deceased parents' home. The police have determined the fire was deliberately caused and they are now treating it as an open homicide case. They are asking anyone

who might have seen anything untoward
or noticed anyone acting suspiciously
early last night to please contact
their local police station."

Shit! Audrey recognized the address and knew it was the David Knowles her sister, Becka, was desperately in love with when their parents died. He was a shit to her at that time. Good riddance, she thought, as she listened to friends and family of the couple say they had no idea who would have wanted them dead. "Such a lovely couple," they said.

CHAPTER
FORTY-THREE

"What do you mean she saw you? Shit! I thought you said you were going to do surveillance. Not picking her up on the beach like some horny stud. What were you thinking?" Higgins was furious.

"Fuck! How did I know she was going to be sitting there just watching me? She crept down the road and scared the living daylights out of me. She has no idea who I am. Do you still want me to continue, or not?" Eric needed the money but wasn't going to beg.

"It might work in our favor. At least you have a reason for contacting her again."

"What reason would that be?"

"To ask her out on a date, dipshit! You're still single and the world's biggest woman magnet, aren't you?"

"She's not really my type. But I guess I could handle a dinner date. As long as you are paying."

"Take it out of your fee, you cheap shit. Call me when you have arranged it." He hung up.

Higgins needed to get into Audrey's office. He was sure she

was hiding something. Where are her mother's pearls? She was wearing them the night her brother died and she hasn't worn them since. Why? Is there a reason? Were the pearls taken the night she was killed? Ripped from her throat by Audrey or her brother?

Did her brother leave a confession? Had Audrey found Greta's blackmailing list? What was Deacon James doing there? Higgins knew everything was connected. But how? He was becoming obsessed with the case. In fact, it wasn't even an official case. All death certificates stated death by natural causes and he was already getting a shitload of flak from the Super. Others in his office thought him crazy. "You need to move on," they would say. "There isn't anything there. You are chasing ghosts." Maybe. Maybe he was. He walked over to his wall, removed the photos and charts and placed them in file boxes. He would take the case home with him… take a couple of days off. He was due for a break.

CHAPTER
FORTY-FOUR

I t was the busiest time of the day. Guests checking out. Cabins to clean. Laundry to do. Audrey didn't like hiring help but today she had no choice. Mary was a local girl with a great work ethic. She had sent her over to start cleaning the cabins while she handled the guests. The phone just didn't stop ringing. She let it go to voicemail while she handled the morning departures. By noon the last guest had left and she headed over to the cabins to collect the dirty laundry. Today she would take the laundry into Mangonui. The service was fast and cheap.

Audrey passed the Motor Camp on her way through Hihi. She thought she saw the good-looking guy from yesterday. He was leaving the little blue camp shop swinging a carton of milk. She almost waved and then thought better of it. Shame. I guess he just wasn't into me.

The little town of Mangonui was buzzing with holiday activity. The Four Square shop housed the local bank and the post office. She saw the local policeman, Detective Constable

Bromley's car parked outside. She thought twice about picking up some supplies. Too late. He spotted her.

"Morning Audrey. Nice day for it." He walked around to her car window. "Been thinking about you. I heard your brother passed away. Sorry to hear about that. And his caregiver. My sympathies."

"Yes. My brother had been ill for some time. Thanks."

"And his caregiver died of a weak heart, I hear?"

"She was old. I guess it was all too much for her." Nothing gets past him. Just as well he didn't know about her uncle's death, too. She didn't need him digging around in her life again.

"Well, have a nice day." Audrey watched the detective drive away before entering the store. *Shit. Was he questioning the deaths? Surely not. Why would he?* It was over a year ago since bodies had washed up on her beach. She was never a suspect – she made sure of that. After all, these were natural deaths.

It wasn't until she returned to Tiromoana that she realized she hadn't checked her voice messages. "Audrey, this is Eric Chapman, we met yesterday on your beach. I know this is awfully presumptuous of me, but I was wondering if you would join me tonight for dinner. I hear the local Thai restaurant in Mangonui is wonderful. I'll try you later. Or, feel free to call me."

Oh shit. Audrey was all in a tither. It had been some time since she had dined with a man, and a good-looking man, at that. In fact, she couldn't even remember being asked out on a date. What to wear? *Maybe my white linen jacket, silk shirt and skinny jeans?* She had inherited her mother's slender legs; unfortunately she had also inherited her ample breasts. Thinking of her mother she decided to wear the pearls. They would look perfect with the jacket. She dialed his number. "Eric, I just picked up your message. I would love to join you for dinner. Yes, seven would be great. I'll see you tonight."

He is such a gentleman, she thought. She looked at the time. She still had heaps of work to do before guests started arriving. Audrey realized she was singing as she carried fresh flowers and wine to the cabins. A full house tonight. Business was good.

CHAPTER
FORTY-FIVE

Higgins decided to take Marcus with him. By the time he had packed all the files in his ute it was almost midday. He knew Eric would be successful keeping Ms. Wetherby occupied for the evening. He made a last-minute check of the house, grabbed his fishing gear and golf clubs and put Marcus in the back seat. Marcus knew never to jump onto the front seats. He had his bed in the back and that was where he stayed. If he were lucky, Higgins would open the back window so he could feel the wind on his face. He knew his drool would spray in the wind. Freedom. Marcus knew when he was a lucky dog.

Higgins used the two-hour drive to contemplate his next move. Given that it was not a legal investigation, but rather a covert operation, he knew that anything he might find out could not be used officially. But Higgins was like a dog with a bone. He knew the Brown women were involved in their parents' murder. Were they also involved in the death of Greta and their Uncle Steve? He never doubted it for a moment.

He stopped in Kerikeri to drop Marcus at the dog kennels.

"Don't worry, old boy. I'll pick you up tomorrow and we can do some serious beach time." Marcus wasn't convinced and pulled at his lead when the nice lady led him away.

Higgins had arranged to stay at the Hihi Motor Camp where Eric was staked out. He knew Audrey would not recognize his black ute. He wore jeans, a cotton shirt and a baseball hat. As he pulled into the camp he saw Eric's jeep parked outside one of the motel units. The camp's office was painted a bright blue. It doubled as a small shop, selling just some essential food items. He grabbed some milk, butter and a loaf of bread and headed to his unit with key in hand.

Eric walked out onto the small patio. "Join me for a beer?"

Higgins looked at the time. It was just on five. "We have time to get in a little fishing. Whatya say?" He placed his supplies in his fridge, joined Eric on the patio and accepted a beer.

"You go ahead. I have some work to do. I told Audrey I would pick her up at seven. If you are going fishing I suggest you walk around to her second beach. There is a track leading up the hill straight to her cottage – that way you do not have to pass the other cabins. You can only access the second beach when the tide is completely out. You are lucky; you have about an hour to reach the beach before the tide turns. I won't bring Audrey back until after ten o'clock. I thought we would take a drive up to the Karikari Peninsula winery for a glass of wine after dinner. That should fill in some time."

Higgins returned to his unit, grabbed his fishing rod, tackle box, vest and a good-sized knapsack. He stopped at the shop and bought some bait. He was planning on catch and release. He was not one for filleting and cleaning fish. He just liked the sport. He only had forty minutes to get to the second beach across a rocky shoreline. He hoped he would make it in time.

CHAPTER
FORTY-SIX

Audrey was on her fifth change. Clothes covered her bed in piles. Everything she owned now looked outdated and frumpy. She wished he hadn't seen her in her yellow sundress. She pulled her straight jeans from the bottom of one of the piles, tried them on for the third time then turned and checked out her butt. She was proud of her body. Six months of no dairy and no sugar had resulted in a more slender version of her previous self. There was nothing she could do with her too ample breasts. Both Honey and she were cursed with their mother's body shape. Deciding on the jeans, she searched for a sexy top and settled for a white silk shirt and navy blue jacket. Standing back she looked in the mirror. Perfect. She removed her mother's pearls from under the diary in her top drawer and clasped them around her neck. That will have to do. She poured herself a glass of wine and waited for the knock at the door.

Beautiful! He was absolutely beautiful! Cream linen trousers and European styled jacket. She couldn't believe her luck. Why me? She could feel her heart beating uncontrollably. Her house key was on the key ring in her car. She seldom locked her cottage. It was so safe in the little seaside town. He took her arm and led her towards his jeep. She looked back at her Rav 4 and wondered if she should have taken the keys out of the car and locked the cottage. Then she remembered her outdoor night vision cameras along the bush tracks. No-one could approach the cottage without being seen. The trappers suggested she use them. Living in a protected kiwi bird zone meant possums, stoats, weasels and rats needed to be eliminated. Audrey preferred to keep an eye on humans.

The Thai restaurant in Mangonui was alive with activity. Audrey never liked noisy restaurants and wished there was an alternative to the crammed quarters and crowded tables. Eric noticed she was uncomfortable.

"Would you sooner we go somewhere quieter?" he asked.

"We could go back to the cottage and I could cook a nice crayfish stir-fry," she offered, a little too enthusiastically.

"Why don't we head up north to Carrington? I can call for reservations on the way. We can sit outside on the terrace overlooking the vineyard where it is quiet. It is such a beautiful night and it is a shame to be inside."

Audrey agreed and he held her chair as she stood up. "You are such a gentleman. Thank you."

At Carrington they ordered grilled fish and salad. The wine was superb and the warm evening breeze smelled of jasmine. The wine made her tipsy. She let him hold her hand.

"Beautiful pearls. I don't think I have ever seen such a unique design."

She felt them with her fingers. "They were my mother's," she said softly.

"Were you close to your mother?

"No. Not really. She died when I was quite young," she said non-committedly.

"Are you close to your father?"

Audrey didn't answer. "I shouldn't be out too late. I have guests in all six cabins and don't like to be gone for too long in case they might need something. She wiped her stained red lips on her serviette and placed it on the plate. "We should be going."

"It is only nine o'clock. It's early yet. Let's have another glass of wine."

"No, thanks. It has been a lovely evening. But, I am a working woman."

Eric called the waiter over and handed him his credit card. As he waited for the receipt, he asked again, "Your father? Are you close to him?"

Audrey was beginning to feel uncomfortable. "Enough talk about me. Tell me about you."

He laughed a belly laugh. "I am an open book. What do you want to know? I went to St Bede's college in Christchurch. Traveled overseas for a couple of years. Backpacked through Europe and then spent a year or so in Canada working at the ski fields. Returned to New Zealand in my late twenties and have mostly run my own companies. I like being independent."

"And you are on holiday here in the far north?"

"Yes, I love fishing and a mate told me about this area. I'm glad I came." He kissed her hand. She blushed.

Eric realized that Audrey wasn't going to divulge her life history. In fact, all evening he had been gently prodding her for information about her family. She skimmed the surface. Nothing substantial. Eric just hoped that Higgins had found what he was looking for.

Audrey excused herself, "I just want to pop into the restroom," she said.

Eric took the opportunity to call Higgins. When he got no answer he left a message. "We are on our way. We will be there in about thirty minutes."

CHAPTER
FORTY-SEVEN

Higgins was pleased he hadn't actually caught any fish. It was pleasurable enough sitting on the protruding rocks with his line in the clear waters below. The waves' rhythmic motion was almost hypnotic. He had removed his shoes and rolled up his trouser legs and waded in the water collecting stones he believed were ancient Maori tools. Each one fit perfectly in his hand with a pointed tip for prizing open shell food. He put them in his backpack and gathered up the rest of his gear.

Looking at his surroundings he chose a dense spot just off Audrey's bush track in which to hide his backpack and then headed up the hill. It was a steep climb but well marked. Over a hundred steps had been chiseled out of the clay cliff. Reaching the top of the ridge he saw the other track leading to the cottage. Eric had described the access so there would be no surprises. He hoped the guests were not wandering around. He was carrying his fishing gear and could pass as any guest returning from the beach.

He was surprised to find the cottage door unlocked. He

called out, "Hello!" No reply. The sun was setting on the horizon and daylight was fading. Her computer needed a password; frustrated, he began a search of the bedside drawers and the large chest of drawers in her bedroom. Pearls, where are the pearls? He saw the notebook. It was Audrey's mother's old diary. Excited, he sat on the bed and began to read. It was all there. He had them!! He had a motive!

He didn't see her coming. The blow to his head was instant and deadly. Detective Constable Higgins crumpled to the floor.

Becka returned the diary to its place in the top drawer of the dresser and poured herself a glass of champagne. She would need to dispose of the body soon. Finding the furniture dolly in the shed, she covered him in old sacks, secured him with ropes and pushed her heavy load out to her car. She returned to collect his fishing rod and tackle box by the front door.

The night was clear and warm. She took the road down to Rocky Beach. It was secluded and not visible from Hihi Township. She wheeled the dolly out to the water's edge. It wasn't easy. The tires caught on the jagged stones. Finally she pulled the body out into the water. She waded up to her waist dragging the body behind her. The tide was going out. She undid the sacks and ropes and released his body into the depths below. She hoped the strong tide would drag him out further into the bay. She threw his rod into the swell and watched it bob in and out of the water. She climbed up onto the large rock and wedged his tackle box in between two large rocks.

Poor detective. "He must have fallen while fishing," they would say. She returned to her car and turned on the radio. She heard the time. It was still early. Protecting the family felt good. He was a nosy shit! She drove off into the dark night.

CHAPTER
FORTY-EIGHT

Audrey was up bright and early. Tiromoana was abuzz with activity. Guests checking out and cabins needing cleaning. Reservations indicated she had a couple of spare cabins that evening. Picking up fresh linens, Audrey headed out into the sunshine. Last night had not been what she expected. She had an uneasy feeling about Eric Chapman. He seemed a little too interested in her life and yet wouldn't confide anything about his. Secretive really. Smarmy. He obviously thought he was God's gift to women. Audrey sighed. She really did prefer women. By lunchtime, cabins were cleaned and guests were busy with their holiday activities.

"Excuse me," Audrey looked up as one of her guests entered her office with a large backpack in hand. "I found this by the track at your Honeymoon beach. It must belong to one of your guests. The beach was deserted so I thought I should bring it to the office."

Audrey looked at the backpack. She had never seen it before. "Where was it?" she asked.

"Tucked behind a big punga as if someone had put it out of

sight. Maybe they had been fishing and then forgot to bring it up with them."

"Thanks. I'll keep it here and see if someone claims it." Audrey waited until the guest left and unzipped the bag to see if there was any form of identification. There was. Shit! There was a wallet with a driver's license.

She would recognize that face anywhere, it belonged to Detective Higgins! She put the wallet in her pocket. There appeared to be some casual clothes, his shaving kit and a few odds and ends. No sign of his badge or anything that would identify him as a policeman. Funny. Obviously not here on police business. Sneaky business, more likely.

Audrey quickly zipped up the bag and put it under the counter. She checked around the cabins and down towards Rocky Beach. He was nowhere to be seen. *Where the hell is he? What was his backpack doing down by my beach?* As she returned to the office, she was surprised to see Eric Chapman standing outside waiting for her.

"I didn't expect to see you so soon," she said as she invited him into the office. "I thought you were taking a fishing cruise today."

"I was. But something has come up. I have to head on back today and wanted to say goodbye and thanks for a lovely evening."

The man looked uneasy. She knew he was lying. "I had a nice time," she lied in return. She had insisted, last night, he need not walk her to the cottage and instead had left him at the top of the driveway, staring at her as she disappeared into the darkness. "Have a safe trip home," she offered as an afterthought.

"I walked up from the camp, and thought I would take the

beach route back. The tide is out and I could do with the exercise."

"By all means," she smiled. "Be my guest. It's a beautiful day." She watched as the tall good-looking man headed across the ridge, past the cabins, towards Rocky Beach. He seemed to have something on his mind.

Audrey now had a dilemma. Should she call the police station and report she had possession of the Detective's backpack or she could do nothing. After all, if she hadn't opened the bag she wouldn't have known it was his anyway. Best let sleeping dogs lie.

CHAPTER
FORTY-NINE

Eric called the Whangarei police station after realizing Higgins bed hadn't been slept in. The office had finally agreed to open his motel room, but there was no sign of Higgins. The room was empty and his car was gone. *Why would he return back to Whangarei and not let me know?* Eric was perturbed. The police said Higgins had taken a couple of days off. "Fishing trip up north," they told him.

There was only one course of action, to retrace his tracks, which he knew led up to Audrey's place. Coming face to face with Audrey was not what he would have chosen to do today. He had already figured out his usual charm was not having the desired effect. In fact, it seemed just the opposite. She seemed annoyed by his obvious interest in her.

Having confirmed Higgins was no longer at Tiromoana, he made his way down Rocky Beach road and onto the rocky shore. It was a beautiful spot and the day was one of the best. Blue skies, clear water and lapping waves were an enticement to strip down and take a quick plunge.

The water was remarkably warm for the usually cool Pacific

Ocean. Eric was a strong swimmer and before long he was swimming out into the bay with long, strong strokes. He lay on his back and looked back at the shore. There was an assortment of small boats and kayaks, mostly fishermen, enjoying the afternoon sun. He could see Audrey's neighbor's house a few hundred meters along the shoreline perched on the edge of a ridge. There was a sandy beach not far from the house and Eric swam in its direction planning on sunning himself on the sand for a while before heading back to the camp.

At first it looked like debris floating in the water until Eric swam closer to the beach and saw it was clothing. His heart missed a beat. Higgins. He just knew it was Higgins. He recognized the jacket immediately. Turning the body over, confirmed his suspicions. He pulled his friend's body onto the shore, sat on the isolated beach and wished he had his cell phone with him. Leaving Higgins above the high tide mark, he made his way up to the house he had seen on the ridge.

CHAPTER
FIFTY

Hihi was inundated with police cars and local fire trucks. The coastguard had been directed to the isolated beach and Higgins's body had been retrieved. Reporters were scrambling to get the news. Locals with cell phones were posting pictures on social media. Drowned. But how could someone just drown in the calm waters of Doubtless Bay? It wasn't until early evening it was reported to be Detective Constable Higgins' body that was found. His car was also located down a track leading to the beach below Audrey Wetherby's property. His fishing tackle box had been retrieved from a nearby beach and a guest at a local cabin resort was interviewed after having found his backpack down by the beach earlier in the day. Had he slipped while fishing off the large rock and hit his head on the rocks below? The police said there would be an enquiry into his death but that, at that time, they did not suspect foul play but rather surmised it was a terrible accident.

Becka watched from her rented beach house on the far side of Hihi Bay, surprised they had recovered his damn body so soon. She was sure it would have washed out to sea. Maybe it had, but the currents had bought it back to shore. Whatever the reason, it was a problem she preferred not to have.

A little background check on the guy who apparently found the body revealed he was a private detective. Becka had seen him talking with the police and had made a few enquiries as to any possible relationship he may have had with Higgins. Her instincts were correct. They were old college friends. She decided to keep an eye on this Eric Chapman. Had Higgins hired him to check on her and her sisters?

She followed the man back to the Hihi Motor Camp where he had booked in for another night. She wondered why he wanted to stay in Hihi. For what purpose? Did he suspect Audrey might be involved?

Becka possessed a collection of passports with various aliases. She had traveled to New Zealand and rented the beach house under an alias. Her new, bright copper red hair, styled in loose curls, replaced her usual straight brown, pageboy haircut. She had used disguises most of her life. This one she liked. It made her feel sexy and desirable. No-one must know she had not left for London. She looked at the yellow sundress and floppy hat she had borrowed from Audrey's cabin the night before.

Audrey always had such good taste. It was a little big, but a belt and padded bra should work just fine. Tomorrow she would put them to good use.

CHAPTER
FIFTY-ONE

Detective Constable Bromley couldn't believe it. Another body in Hihi Bay. Shit! What the fuck was going on? This time a colleague. He had talked to him only a few days ago. Higgins had been chasing up an old double-murder case and Bromley was shocked to find out that it was Audrey Wetherby's parents who had been murdered. She was just a teenager at the time and yet Higgins was sure the children were responsible for their murder. Of course he had no proof and had been told by the Super to leave it alone and move on to more urgent cases. Bromley wondered if Higgins had been up at Audrey's doing a covert investigation under the guise of a fishing trip. The death of Audrey's brother seems to have stirred him up. What had he found out?

Bromley knew it was time to take a drive up to Audrey's and have a word with her. He looked at the time – it was almost lunchtime. All morning he had been at the Whangarei station. So many questions unanswered. He would make it back to Hihi by two. He had asked for the cold case files on the Brown case and was surprised to find that they were no longer in Higgins' office. A team had been sent to his home to look for anything that might indicate that he was suicidal and they discovered all of the Brown case files in his home office. Boxes of reports, photos, slides and newspaper clippings were emptied and sorted into piles on his desk. The home was immaculate. Too immaculate. Colleagues had located his dog. You would never know a dog lived in the home – he must have made the dog wear slippers and a bib.

After loading all the Brown files into the trunk of his car, Bromley made his way north. It was pure curiosity that enticed him to collect the files. Audrey Wetherby's life seemed to attract murder and he was interested to know more about the childhood tragedy that had undoubtedly shaped her life.

Tomorrow he would take a look through the files. He knew her brother had recently passed away. And his caregiver. Strange, that.

CHAPTER
FIFTY-TWO

Audrey finally had a moment to herself. It had been a crazy morning. What was worse, she now had reporters staying in her cabins. They had checked in last night after the commotion on finding the detective's body on the beach. They had even interviewed the bloody guest who had found the backpack and had run to the office after hearing about the body being washed up, yelling. "It must be his! The backpack, it must have been his! That is why it wasn't collected!" She had given the backpack to him, and he had rushed off in his car to hand it over to the police on the Hihi beachfront.

Today the press was scrambling over the rocks taking videos of the location and questioning local fisherman and residents of the small township. Of course, no-one knew anything, except for the owners of the Motor Camp who said that Higgins had checked in the night before and had a friend staying there too.

Audrey realized the friend must have been Eric Chapman. Now it all made sense. But how did Higgins end up in the bay? Had Eric taken her to dinner so that Higgins could snoop around her cottage? Had Higgins made it inside her cottage?

Shit! She checked the dresser and breathed in relief to find the diary was still in the top drawer.

It was time to check the outdoor video cams on the ridge to Honeymoon Beach. She wished she had placed some down at Rocky Beach. Maybe she should get a proper video surveillance system set up at Tiromoana. But then again, it might be better to leave things as they were.

As she returned from the ridge with the memory cards from the cams, she heard a car pulling up. Damn. She turned towards the car park and saw Detective Bromley stepping out of his police car. She waved. *Shit! What does he want?* She put the cards in her pocket and went to greet him. "Detective Bromley, what a surprise. What can I do for you?"

CHAPTER
FIFTY-THREE

Honey and Matt were spending the day together. Honey checked her email while catching up on the latest news online. "Hey, Matt!" she called. "Detective Higgins was found dead in Hihi Bay. Shit! We should call Audrey."

Matt leaned over Honey and read the article on the screen. "It says they have not determined the cause of death. They don't say he drowned. He must have not had any water in his lungs. I wonder how he ended up washed up in Audrey's bay. You should call her."

Honey had not spoken to Audrey since she left Tiromoana. They had all agreed to distance themselves from the recent deaths in the family. Especially because Detective Higgins was obsessed with proving they had something to do with their parents' death.

"I think I should drive up and see if there is anything we can do. Audrey must be beside herself. Can you come too?" she asked.

"I can't get away right now. But you should go. I'll look after the cats," Matt offered.

Honey stuffed clothes in a suitcase, grabbed her laptop, kissed Matt and the cats goodbye and headed off north. She wondered if she should call the others but decided she should wait until she'd talked to Audrey. Audrey would know what to do.

Matt watched her car disappear down the road and returned to Honey's office desk. He knew her password for her desktop computer and he began his search.

CHAPTER
FIFTY-FOUR

He was walking up the ridge. The outdoor cam took three photos in succession and there was no doubt, Detective Higgins had taken the track from Honeymoon Beach. Video cams positioned up the clay bank and along the top ridge caught him walking towards her cottage.

But there were no photos of Higgins returning to Honeymoon Beach. Audrey had a bad feeling that Detective Higgins didn't make it out of Tiromoana alive. This time she knew she was in serious trouble, and what made it worse was that she wasn't even responsible for his death. But who was?

Without a doubt she would be the first person they would suspect. Once the police went through her father's slides they would know she and her sisters had been molested. They would think she had a motive for her parents' murder. But why would she kill the detective and leave all the evidence in the hands of the police? One thing was for sure: Eric Chapman would not be her number-one supporter. His visit was obviously to search for any sign of the detective. He must have known the detective had been at Tiromoana the night he went missing. Did he suspect she had something to do with his disappearance?

She had been surprised to see Detective Bromley. He said he was just making a routine call to see if she had any information relating to Detective Higgins. She had explained she had not seen him at Tiromoana and a guest had found his backpack down at Honeymoon Beach. She presumed he was fishing off the rocks down there. No. She had no idea what he was doing in Hihi. The last time she had seen him was last week. He had come to talk to Matt Walters about Greta's fortune-telling scams. Apparently some church members had been complaining.

"Just thought I would let you know that I am taking over your parents' cold case. I know Higgins was working on it prior to his death. I'll let you know if I have any questions," Bromley had informed her.

Audrey knew it was just a matter of time before he discovered what her father's slides revealed. She would need to produce solid evidence that Ben had been responsible for both murders. She set to work. Now that Detective Bromley was on the case, she didn't have much time.

CHAPTER
FIFTY-FIVE

Honey flopped down on Audrey's huge settee sinking into its feathery depths. "I can't believe it! He was found down by your beach? What the heck was he doing here? Did you see him? Did you talk to him?"

Audrey explained she was out with Eric Chapman the night Higgins went missing. She'd returned after nine o'clock and gone straight to bed. The next morning a guest found Higgins' backpack down by Honeymoon Beach. She didn't know if she should tell Honey about the video cam.

"So you think this Eric Chapman and Detective Higgins were in on it together? Do you suppose they had a fight and he killed him?" Honey asked hopefully.

"I wish that was the case," said Audrey. "But somehow I don't think so."

"Then who? Who would have killed him? You don't really think he just fell off a rock, hit his head and toppled into the bay?"

"I have no idea. But Detective Bromley from our local Mangonui Police Station has taken over our parents' case and once he looks at the slides, he is sure to think we had something to do with it."

"Maybe it is time to tell them that Ben was responsible for their deaths. After all, he is dead now and the police will leave us alone," Honey suggested.

Audrey liked this suggestion. "We should ask Simone and Becka first. If they agree then I think that is the best decision we could make." She handed Honey a glass of champagne. "Let's make a toast to closing our parents' murder case for good."

"Cheers," they said in unison.

"To Mum and Dad, may they never rest in peace," Audrey added.

"Ditto," said Honey.

CHAPTER
FIFTY-SIX

H e was surprised to see Audrey and a rather lovely
blonde woman entering the police station.

"What can I do for you, ladies?" Detective
Bromley asked as he escorted them into his back office.

"I am Audrey's sister, Honey Brown," Honey introduced
herself as she took a seat in front of his desk. "We have some
information pertaining to our parents' murder and thought it
time that we shared it with you. I understand you have taken
over the case."

"I don't suppose you have had a chance to review the files
yet?" Audrey asked.

"There is a lot of information to go through. I imagine it
will take me a few days to review it all," he replied, removing a
notepad and pen from a pile of papers on his desk. "So what
information do you wish to share?"

Honey began first. She explained the abuse she had suffered
at the hands of her parents, her father in particular. The detective was shocked and appalled. Honey continued to explain
what had happened the day of her parents' murder. How her

brother, Ben, had walked in on her father molesting her and how he had reacted. Honey said Ben told her to leave and go to the park. She didn't return until the police arrived. She presumed that Ben had murdered her parents.

"And you, Audrey?" the detective asked, "Were you there that day?"

"Yes," she replied quietly. "I came home to find that my brother had stabbed my father. There was blood everywhere. He told me to go. I was scared and went for a ride on my bike. I didn't come back until after I heard the police sirens."

Honey was visibly shocked. Audrey had never said she was in the house just after Ben had killed their father.

"Did your brother also kill your mother?" The detective couldn't believe what he was hearing.

"Our sister, Becka, told us that she arrived home and found both our father and mother already dead. Like us, she didn't return until the police arrived at our house. Our eldest sister, Simone, took us to stay at her flat that night. We didn't talk to the police until the following day.

"We never told them Ben had killed our parents. Our parents had abused us all, and Ben was only trying to protect us." Honey started to sob. "We were just happy they couldn't hurt us any more."

"Where is your sister, Becka, now?"

"She is in London," Honey replied. "She came back for Ben's funeral but returned to London a few days ago.

"I would like her contact information so I can verify her account of the events," the detective said as he continued to write notes on his scratchpad. "Is this the first time you have told anyone about this?"

"Yes," said Audrey. "Now our brother is dead, we felt that it was time to tell the truth. We know Detective Higgins was working on our parents' case before his awful accident. We just want to help you close the case for him."

The detective had the Brown sisters sign their written statements and thanked them for their help. "It must be difficult for you to dredge up these awful memories," he said gratefully.

"Yes," said Audrey. "It is. Hopefully this puts an end to it now and we can put it all behind us."

CHAPTER
FIFTY-SEVEN

I t was all there. Higgins' notes were impeccable. Every tiny detail marked with sticky notes. Detective Bromley looked at the circled crime photo of three schoolbags hanging on wooden pegs inside the front entrance and read Higgins' notes:

Three schoolbags belonging to Honey, Audrey and Becka.
Proves they were in the home before the police arrived.
Were they responsible for the murders?

Bromley opened the box of Kodak carousel slides. The top carousel had post-its with more notes:

Proof the three sisters were all molested by their father
and uncle.
Who was taking the photos? Their mother?
Proves motive for murder.

The detective held up the slides to the light, one by one,

and knew that what the Brown sisters had told him was the truth. They had been molested. Ben Brown, the brother, was strangely absent. At least he was not present in the slides Higgins had marked. Was it true he was responsible for the murders? Was knowing that his sisters were being abused by his father and mother enough for him to snap and commit the murders as his sisters had described? Bromley sat back in his chair and sighed. He would need to call his Supervisor. The Brown murder was one of the biggest unsolved murders in New Zealand. It would be all over the news.

Bromley was not a stranger to the limelight. Too many murders had taken place in his territory over the past few years. At least these murders had taken place a long way from home.

He saw a manila folder marked "Eric Chapman/Audrey Wetherby" and began to read its contents.

Sunday: Report – Eric to survey AW in Hihi
Unexpected liaison on AW beachfront
Eric establishes a connection.
Monday night: Meet Eric at Hihi Motor Camp 5.30
Eric dinner with AW 7–10 p.m.

More random notes:

Audrey wearing her mother's pearls the night of Ben's death?
Greta Baywater. Proof she scammed church members and kept
records of her meetings – need to find
her notes – Ben confession? Murder?
Steve Brown – Uncle – Murdered?

The detective realized Higgins' visit to Hihi was not, in fact, a fishing trip but instead a covert investigation of Audrey. Why?

Bromley needed to talk to Eric Chapman. Did he know something about Higgins' death?

Now it was all making sense. Audrey Wetherby must have known Higgins' had found proof that they were involved in their parents' murders. Had Audrey and her sister simply pre-empted a forthcoming interrogation based on the new evidence? Now blaming their brother seemed a little too convenient. After all, he was dead and unable to defend himself.

And he wasn't the only one who had died recently. Ben's caregiver, Greta Baywater, Audrey's uncle and now Higgins were all dead. Were all these deaths related? Had Higgins discovered proof that they had been murdered? By whom? Audrey? Why did he suspect Audrey?

He picked up the phone and started making calls. This was big. He would need to get his facts right before contacting the Super.

CHAPTER
FIFTY-EIGHT

Yesterday, Becka had received an email from Audrey asking her to contact her immediately. She had not been returning any phone calls in order to keep her presence in New Zealand a secret. Thinking she was back in London was better for everyone concerned and it allowed her complete anonymity while she planned her next move.

Keeping in mind today's digital forensics, she was careful to place the call from a landline using an old-fashioned phone with no caller ID. She had agreed with Honey and Audrey to confess to the police their knowledge that their brother had committed the murders. She didn't want anyone nosing around in her private life and hopefully this would put an end to her sisters' constant harassment by the local police.

She just had one more loose end to take care of and he was sitting at the next table to her deep in conversation with a man. Chapman was good-looking. Obviously successful with women. She had watched him eyeing the women as they walked by the little Mangonui waterfront café. Becka hoped her new vibrant red hair, revealing neckline and renewed confidence would entice him into an encounter.

When his guest left the table, Chapman looked over her way. "Lovely day," he commented. "Are you visiting, or a local?"

"Just visiting," she replied giving him a smile. "And you?"

"Just here for the fishing. Heading back tomorrow."

"I've heard there are some great fishing spots around here. Don't suppose you could give me a few tips?" she asked provocatively.

"Actually, I am taking a boat out this afternoon. I don't suppose you would like to join me?" he said, walking over to join her at her table.

"Why, that would be wonderful. But I'm not really dressed for fishing," she laughed pointing to her high-heeled sandals and yellow sundress.

"You look perfectly dressed to me," he said. "I have rented a nineteen-footer for the afternoon and I would love you to join me. I promise I'll take good care of you. I am a gentleman," he said convincingly.

"I'm sure you are." She laughed. "Why not? I could do with some fresh sea air."

"Shall we?" He stood up, putting out his hand as she rose from the table.

Becka was grateful for her large sunglasses and wide-brimmed sun hat. She was sure no-one would recognize her as she accompanied the man to the Mangonui wharf.

Once on board, he offered her a glass of cold champagne. Becka smiled. She couldn't have planned this better. Just the two of them. Heading out to sea on a beautiful sunny afternoon. A warm breeze, calm waters and a good-looking man. What a shame she couldn't keep him. He might be a perfect gentleman, but she was no innocent lady.

CHAPTER
FIFTY-NINE

Audrey and Honey returned to Tiromoana, relieved it was over. "Poor Ben," said Honey. "He kept it a secret his whole life and as soon as he died, we broke our promise and now the whole world will know what he did."

Audrey agreed, but said, "We really had no choice, Honey. The police now have all the evidence they need to say we had a motive. Even if they couldn't prove anything, they would never leave us alone."

"I know you are right. I just wish we didn't have to drag it all up again. It feels as if it all happened yesterday. All the memories, the abuse..." Honey picked up her overnight bag. "I am heading home. Matt is looking after the cats. He has been such a darling. So supportive. I am lucky to have him in around. I don't know what I would have done without him."

Audrey watched Honey drive away in her little red convertible and returned to her office. She had been neglecting her business over the past few days. Dealing with the police snooping around had been a full-time job. Now she could get back to work. She took her laptop outside to the picnic table overlooking the bay. A powerboat was heading across the bay towards the open sea. In the distance she could just make out a couple. A man and a woman in a large yellow sun hat. Audrey wished she had someone to share the afternoon with. She watched them until they disappeared out of sight.

Looking at the bookings on her screen she sighed. More reporters from television and newspapers. Would they never give up? At least it was great for business. The death of Detective Higgins was a constant highlight on the evening news. No water in his lungs. It was either an awful accident or someone wanted him dead. Everyone had an opinion. The police were being tight lipped. "Still under investigation" was all they would say.

Audrey half expected Eric Chapman to make another appearance. She felt stupid for having thought that he was interested in her, when in fact he was just getting paid to snoop on her. Shit! Higgins' death might be inconvenient under the circumstances, but hell, she was pleased he was dead. Shame Eric couldn't take the same route.

She looked up as a guest approached her. "I don't suppose you knew Detective Higgins by any chance?"

Bloody reporters! "No. Can't say I knew him. Sorry." She stood up and returned inside.

She watched the reporter walk away. She wasn't actually lying. After all, she didn't actually know Higgins. Meeting him a couple of times doesn't warrant any familiarity.

She was pleased her last name wasn't Brown. As soon as Detective Bromley filed his report, her parents' murder case would be all over the news. Solving one of the biggest cold cases in New Zealand's history would soon take the attention away from Higgins' death. She made a mental note to ask the detective if her and her sisters' names could be kept private. No harm in asking.

CHAPTER
SIXTY

Matt Walters cared about Honey. Ever since Detective Higgins had told him Honey's parents were murdered thirty years ago and he was reopening the case, Matt had been worried for her. What was the new evidence? Was it something to do with the slides Higgins had mentioned? He wished he had asked him. Probed him further.

Upon their return, Honey wouldn't talk about it. But Matt was curious. A search on her computer revealed nothing. But an online search of the thirty-year-old murder revealed much more. It was all there. Photos of Honey's parents smiling and looking happy. Photos of the 1950 bungalow where the family lived at the time of the murders. What was most disturbing was the lack of suspects or even a motive. The children were interviewed. They had no alibis but told the police they were not at home at the time of the murders. The son, Ben, who was twenty-one at the time was the main person of interest. But why? Is that why the death of Ben was of so much interest to the police? One of the sisters was also a person of interest. Which sister? Audrey? Becka? Honey?

Honey seemed so innocent, so vulnerable. Surely she had nothing to do with it, but her sisters were another matter. Had Higgins found proof that Ben had killed his parents? Or worse, was the whole family involved?

Shit! Why didn't I probe him further? Now he is dead. Matt had a horrible feeling. Had Higgins been murdered too?!

His phone buzzed in his pocket. He looked at the caller ID but didn't recognize the number.

"Hello, Matt Walters," he answered. It was Detective Bromley from the Mangonui Police Station. Matt listened to what the detective had to say.

"You want permission to exhume my aunt's body? Why? I see, detective. Yes, of course." Matt was surprised by the request.

After a lengthy conversation, Matt hung up the phone and realized there was more to his aunt's death than he had imagined.

Matt told the detective about Audrey finding his aunt's diary, which she had given to Deacon James at his request. The detective seemed to know about his aunt's blackmailing tactics but was surprised to learn about the diary. The conversation troubled Matt.

He looked at the time. Honey was returning soon. He had cooked her favorite meal, chicken curry and rice. He was chilling a nice wine. She said that she had something to tell him. What, he wondered.

CHAPTER
SIXTY-ONE

It was seven o'clock before Becka and Eric returned to the Mangonui dock. She knew Eric had enjoyed their afternoon at sea. He had suggested dinner and didn't take much convincing that dinner at her place would be preferable.

A quick stop at the Mangonui Four Square shop to pick up supplies and she was back at her beachfront rental house in Hihi. Becka had time for a hot bath before Eric would return to join her for dinner and drinks.

Becka loved classical music and had quite a collection on her laptop. Bach's Orchestral Suite #3 in D played in the background as she soaked in bubbles and planned her evening. The planning was as exciting as the execution. She knew some people liked to gamble, sky jump or have affairs to break the monotony of their mundane lives. Becka liked the adrenalin rush of getting away with murder.

She was careful never to leave behind any trace evidence. Tomorrow she knew she would need to take the remaining evidence with her – away from Hihi, away from the far north.

She would make a stop on a country road on her way to Auckland airport. Her flight to Heathrow was scheduled to leave at 10.30 p.m. She would have a good twenty-four hours to do what she needed to do.

Dressed in a sexy red dress and sporting her vibrant new red hair, Becka poured a glass of chilled Oyster Bay sauvignon blanc and dribbled oil and vinegar dressing over her freshly made salad.

CHAPTER
SIXTY-TWO

Eric Chapman was a selfish bastard. He told himself this as he prepared for a night of sex and debauchery. He should be digging up information on his mate's untimely death. Instead, he was choosing what shirt to wear to impress the beautiful redhead he had the hots for. He knew she was older than he was, but she looked ten years younger. She had a figure to die for: slender, petite and such a tiny waist. And that red hair and those green eyes! She said her name was Angel, and an angel she was. She reminded him of someone but he couldn't think who it was. That yellow dress looked familiar, too.

With his fishing gear in the trunk, he threw his bag and laptop in the back seat. He was pretty sure he would be staying the night with Angel so it would save him coming back to pack. Tomorrow he would get back to work. First on his list was Audrey Wetherby. Higgins' last confirmed location was on her beach. Eric knew Higgins had been searching her cottage that night. Was he still there when he dropped Audrey off? Did she find him going through her stuff and kill him? Eric just had to prove it. He had reported his suspicions to Detective Bromley only this morning. The detective had called to confirm Higgins had hired him to keep an eye on Audrey Wetherby. He was surprised to hear Higgins had kept notes on their association. However, the detective was shocked to learn that Higgins had been planning to check out Audrey's cottage while Eric was wining and dining her. An illegal search was obviously not something Bromley approved of.

Eric expected Audrey Wetherby would be taken in for questioning. With any luck he could gain access to her cottage and finish what Higgins had started.

Proof is what he needed. Proof Audrey had something to hide. A motive. Anything. Then it came to him. The yellow dress. Audrey was wearing a similar dress the afternoon he met her on the beach. He laughed. The two women couldn't be more different.

He pulled into the driveway of the expensive two-storied home overlooking the Hihi Park and waterfront. Angel was on the balcony. "Come on up," she called. "I have just put the crayfish on the BBQ."

Eric's thoughts of murder and mayhem dissipated into the warm ocean breeze as he climbed the steps to the balcony.

CHAPTER
SIXTY-THREE

A udrey could sense something was not right. She could smell trouble. Baring their souls to Detective Bromley should have deflected any suspicion away from her but it seemed as though whatever she did, she could not shake the feeling of pending doom.

The death of Detective Higgins was troublesome. She wondered if he had been in her cottage the night of his death. She wished she had been more observant when she returned her pearls to her dresser. Her mother's diary was in the wooden box and she didn't see anything unusual. But she had noticed her computer was turned off. She always just put her computer to sleep and had presumed that there had been a power cut while she was out. She checked with the power company but they didn't have any record of a power cut. Had Higgins tried to access her computer? Had he been inside the cottage?

She wondered if she should come clean to Detective Bromley and show him the night cam displaying Higgins walking up the ridge from Honeymoon Beach towards the cottage and the cabins. But there was no record of him leaving

Tiromoana,. That could be more incriminating, as she had no alibi after 9 o'clock, which, she learned, was approximately the estimated time of his demise.

What made matters worse was Eric Chapman. He could prove he dropped her off at home shortly after nine-thirty. She doubted any of her guests could vouch for her, as the cottage was not visible from the cabins on the ridge. She was surprised Eric had not visited her today. She was sure he would be on her case. Maybe he had given up. She hoped so.

She didn't have to worry about Greta's death.

She was buried six feet under, and her Uncle Steve had been cremated. It was just bloody Higgins' death that was haunting her.

Her sisters were all in agreement they should confide in the police that Ben had carried out their parents' murders. She expected tomorrow the world would know. What was worse, most of the media were still in Hihi covering the death of Higgins. Would her name be exposed? Would she suddenly be put in the spotlight? Audrey was on her third glass of wine. Wine was not going to make this go away. Shit. Shit. Shit.

Then Audrey decided to take control of the situation. She collected her mother's diary, her photocopies of Greta's note-book, a full bottle of wine and made her way across the ridge to the Kiwi Cabin. The guest staying there was a recognized TV personality. It was time to tell her story.

CHAPTER
SIXTY-FOUR

Breakfast was a sacred time in the Bromley household. It was a time when Bromley could sit with the family and catch up on his three daughters' lives and share some quality time with his wife, Mary. This morning they had the news playing quietly on the big screen TV in the adjoining lounge.

> "Audrey Wetherby, daughter of Murray and Sophie Brown who were murdered in their Christchurch home over thirty years ago has told our own TV One's David Doherty that it was her brother who committed the crimes."

Detective Constable Bromley, shocked, turned towards the TV as the familiar broadcaster's face appeared on the screen.

> "Ms. Wetherby advised she has kept quiet all these years out of respect

for her brother, Ben Brown. His passing last week released her and her sisters from their promise of silence. Ms. Wetherby and her sisters have given written statements to the police identifying their brother as the perpetrator of the crimes. Ms. Wetherby explained that she and her sisters were constantly abused by their parents and that Ben had snapped when witnessing this abuse and committed the crimes with the sole purpose of protecting his siblings.

Ms. Wetherby found her mother's diary and Ben's confessions of his crime among her brother's belongings, and she has shared this evidence with TV One. Full details will follow in tonight's six o'clock news."

And there was more. David Doherty continued,

"Ms. Wetherby also confided to me another disturbing matter. Her brother, Ben Brown's, caregiver, Greta Baywater who died the same night as Brown, at seventy-two years of age, apparently had her own sordid past. Ms. Wetherby found evidence in her brother's home that Greta Baywater was bribing members of her church in order to keep silent about their discussions

held during Greta's fortune-telling sessions. Ms. Wetherby found a notebook belonging to Ms. Baywater, which contained details of these discussions. We understand the police are aware of this situation. We will keep you updated as more information comes to hand."

"Bloody hell!" Bromley was pissed off. "What has the woman done? I have to go." He grabbed his jacket and headed for the station. He hadn't even finished his report.

Bloody Audrey had pre-empted him. She was clever. She was covering all her bases.

He didn't have to wait to reach his office before his cell phone started ringing furiously. It was the Super. "What the fuck, Bromley! Did you know about this?"

"I interviewed Audrey Wetherby and her sister yesterday but I still had some loose ends to tie up before I finished my report. I will get it to you this morning."

"Too right you will! I'm coming up to see you. What is all this about the bloody caregiver? Did you know she was black-mailing her parish members? Have you seen this so-called, note-book evidence?"

"No, I have never seen a notebook. Didn't know about it until this morning. Some of the members of the Baywater woman's church made accusations about her demanding money. I have arranged to have her body exhumed. We should know in a couple of days if her death was caused by anything other than natural causes."

"I want to see your report on the Brown case as soon as I get there. This is big, Bromley. One of the biggest unsolved crimes in the country and you get a confession and don't bother to pick up the phone and discuss it with me. You'd better have a good explanation. I can't believe bloody David Doherty didn't call us for a comment prior to airing this!"

Bromley knew he was in deep shit. Fuck! He checked his messages and there was a message left at midnight last night from Doherty.

"Detective Bromley, David Doherty TV One here, I will be breaking the story on the Browns' murder tomorrow morning. Audrey Wetherby met with me tonight and has filled me in on her statement to you today. If you have any comment, please call me. It will be going to air at eight. Also, I understand you are looking into Greta Baywater's death. If possible, I would like a comment on this case, too."

Double shit!

CHAPTER
SIXTY-FIVE

As Audrey was sitting in the Kiwi cabin spilling her guts to David Doherty, Becka was wiping her fingerprints off every surface in the holiday house. Eric had been kind enough to help her with the dishes after dinner. He even cleaned the BBQ, for which she was extremely grateful. He was now lying on the sofa wrapped in plastic like a shiny chrysalis. Cleanliness was important to Becka. Cleanliness and attention to detail were her two strongest attributes.

It was almost midnight. The streets in the small seaside township were deserted. She hadn't heard a car in over an hour. The nearby motor camp was full of campervans and kids. The kids would be fast asleep and the parents were either drinking or had passed out watching TV in their metal cocoons. She looked out the window. The night sky was spectacular. The Milky Way was a banquet of stars, luminous shapes and wisps of white. A pale moon shone brightly, reflecting in the still waters of Hihi Bay. Becka had forgotten how wonderful the New Zealand night sky was. London lights blocked out the night sky. She would miss this.

Finally she was packed, with all her luggage in Eric's Jeep. She had returned her rental car in Mangonui before lunch and had been grateful for Eric's offer to drive her back to Hihi. She was even more grateful she had the use of his ute for the four-hour drive back to Auckland. Now wasn't that kind of him?

She backed up the Jeep Wrangler to the front door and opened its back door. Becka was small but strong.

Even so, she needed to place him on a blanket and slide him across the clean wooden floor to the door.

Levering him head-first then hoisting his legs up into the Jeep, she managed to lay him neatly beside their luggage. She was pleased to see he had conveniently bought his luggage with him. Men! Always come prepared for an overnight stay. Gotta love 'em.

She locked the door, placed the key under the mat, as she had been instructed by the landlord, and returned to the Jeep. Pulling the driver's seat forward, she turned on the ignition and heard the motor roar into life. The radio was tuned to the National Radio Station. They were playing Mozart by the London Symphony Orchestra. Perfect. She sat back and headed into the night. She just had one stop to make on the way before she headed out onto the main highway.

CHAPTER
SIXTY-SIX

udrey heard the police cars entering her driveway. They looked pissed off as they strode up the path to her cottage office.

"Detective Bromley," she acknowledged him as he burst open the door.

"You know Inspector Burt?" Bromley snapped. She nodded. "We understand you have some evidence relating to your brother's death, your parents' murder and Greta Baywater's blackmailing activities. We would have appreciated you divulging this information to the police rather than having it blabbed all over the morning news. What were you thinking?"

"I wasn't thinking!" Audrey exclaimed guiltily. "I had been drinking last night. I was so upset with everything. Dragging up the past." She sniffed. "I knew it would be all over the news soon enough and just wanted to tell my side of the story. David Doherty was staying in one of my cabins and he was so nice and seemed to really care about me. I guess it all just came out. I am so sorry. I will get you the diary and notebook." Audrey left the office and the two policemen followed her into her cottage.

Handing over the evidence, Audrey explained, "I took a photocopy of Greta's notebook before handing the original to Deacon James. He said he would burn the evidence to protect him and his fellow parishioners.

"I got a strange vibe from Deacon James and that's why I decided to photocopy the notebook before giving it to him. I just had this funny feeling that maybe he had something to do with Greta Baywater's death. When you read what she knew about him, you might think that, too."

Detective Bromley's demeanor softened slightly with Audrey's explanation of the situation. "Thank you, Audrey. But why didn't you tell me about your mother's diary?" The detective was skimming the pages and was obviously shocked at its contents.

"Because it was awful, what she wrote," she explained. My brother must have kept it all these years. Now you can understand why he did what he did."

Detective Bromley handed the diary to the Inspector. "This pretty much says it all," he said flipping through the pages. "Thank you Audrey, we'll let you know if we need to talk to you again. By the way, I haven't been able to get in touch with your sister, Becka. If you are talking to her can you ask her to contact the station? Just have to verify the statement you gave."

"Will do, detective." Audrey watched them go and let out a deep sigh. All was going to plan. All suspicion was now focusing on Ben and Deacon James. She still didn't have any idea how she would deflect any suspicion regarding the death of Detective Higgins. Hopefully they would be too distracted with what they already had on their plates. At least she had some breathing time.

She looked at the time. Shit! She still had a couple of cabins to clean. More reporters were due in this afternoon. She knew the press would now hound her and her sisters. At least Becka was out of the country.

She doubted they would be able to track down Simone. She had managed to erase any record of her previous life prior to her marriage. As for Honey, Audrey knew she should call her and explain why she had done what she had.

She wasn't looking forward to it. Honey didn't deserve this. She would suggest she leave the country for a while. Maybe go and stay with Becka in London. Yes. Perfect idea. She picked up the phone to make the call.

CHAPTER
SIXTY-SEVEN

Honey and Matt had watched the morning news in horror. "What the hell made Audrey tell all?" Honey sobbed uncontrollably. "Now everyone will know. I can't believe she told them about your aunt, Matt. I am so sorry."

Matt was quiet. He was silently pissed off that Audrey hadn't told him she had kept a copy of his aunt's notebook. He didn't trust Audrey. Not for one minute. She was definitely hiding something. But what?

"She must have had her reasons." He paused. "I don't think you should go to work today. Ring and tell them you have the flu. Don't worry, Honey, we will work this out."

Honey had told Matt the full story. He was appalled at what Honey had gone through as a child. Now she would have to deal with the aftermath of what Audrey had done. Matt knew she needed some time alone. He kissed her goodbye and left her on the sofa covered in fluffy cats and pillows.

Audrey called to say she had purchased Honey a ticket for the 10.30 p.m. flight to Heathrow that night.

"You should leave the country until all of this blows over," Audrey had told her. "If the police have any questions, they can talk to you over there. I can handle everything here. After all, it was me that caused all of this. A break away will do you the world of good. Why don't you suggest to Matt that he comes with you?"

Honey looked around her apartment. She had nothing here to stay for. Even her cats seemed to be getting used to her absence. Audrey was right. She must go. Go before the press found her. "I'll go," she said. Can you let Becka know I am on my way? See if she can pick me up from the airport? I have to pack. Shit. I hope I have enough warm clothes. It will be cold as hell over there."

"I'll email you through the e-ticket. I suggest you don't answer your phone. It will most likely be reporters. I will be the spokesperson for the family so you don't have to answer any questions. I'll keep you out of this, Honey." Audrey hung up and left Honey in a packing frenzy.

With her suitcase finally packed and the cats in their cage, Honey waited for Matt to drive her to the airport. She had begged him to accompany her but he said he would join her in London in a few days. "I need a couple of days to tie things up here," he had explained.

CHAPTER
SIXTY-EIGHT

Becka opened the front door of Eric Chapman's messy house. "How can anyone live like this?" she thought as she walked through the kitchen looking for the inside entrance to the garage. Opening the garage doors, she parked the Ute inside and closed the doors immediately. She had been careful to wear one of Eric's shirts and tuck her red hair neatly inside one of his baseball caps. If any neighbors saw the Jeep returning home, they would presume he was driving. Details. It was all in the details.

Once inside, Becka set to work. Pills, booze and pot were everywhere, throughout the house. Setting the stage for an overdose was easier than she thought. With Eric unwrapped and redressed in casual jeans and sweatshirt, she propped him appropriately against the sofa, unpacked his suitcase and returned his fishing gear to the shelf in the garage.

All evidence in the Jeep was wiped clean. Even though she was wearing gloves and a hat she didn't want to risk anything. One stray hair could lead to detection. She made sure she returned the driver's seat to its original position.

She checked the time. It was almost six a.m. She had a full day before her flight left tonight for London. She was getting tired and knew she needed to get some sleep. She took one last look around the house. Perfect.

Changing into running shoes, black sweats and a black hoodie, she ran three miles to where she had hidden her luggage in dense bush. She used a new SIM card to order a taxi and immediately replaced it with another. The call would never be traced.

The taxi dropped her at an airport hotel where she collapsed on the bed and slept soundly until her wake up call at 6 p.m. Becka liked her new look. The red hair changed her appearance considerably. She chose her favorite black knee-high boots, tight black pants and checkered blazer. A multi-colored silk scarf and dark glasses added to her disguise. I might even keep this look when I return to London, she thought. But knew she shouldn't take any chances. When they find Eric's body, people would say he was with a redhead either at lunch or on the boat. Mangonui was a small town and she knew they would have been spotted. It was definitely time to leave New Zealand.

She checked in early, went through security and spent the next hour browsing the duty-free shops. She reached the gate to find a large crowd had gathered waiting to board. Traveling business class, she had timed it perfectly. She handed the flight attendant her passport and boarding pass and with a flick of her pretty red hair walked the gangway to the Boeing 777.

From her window seat she watched as luggage and food carts buzzed to and fro across the tarmac. She ordered a glass of champagne and ignored the long stream of boarding passengers who were accompanying her on her journey back to London.

CHAPTER
SIXTY-NINE

Matt and Honey arrived at the airport at eight o'clock. It was a busy night at the Auckland International Airport and Matt helped Honey drag her heavy suitcase up to the ticket counter. He even paid her $120.00 overweight baggage fee. Air New Zealand was strict on their designated weight limit of 23 kg or 50 lb per passenger. He kissed her goodbye and watched her disappear through security. She was on her own now. The wait at the screening area was long and tedious. When she finally reached the gate, they had just started boarding the coach. She was seated in Row 47C, an aisle seat. Honey was always worried about climbing over other passengers to get to the bathroom in the middle of the night. She hoped no-one was sitting in the middle seat so she would have more room.

She lined up patiently in the gangway with her fellow passengers. She wished she could afford to fly first class or even business class, just once. But Audrey had paid for the ticket and she was just grateful for any seat. Finally she reached the entrance of the plane and was greeted by two smiling attendants who asked her where she was seated. They pointed her down the first aisle. It was difficult with her carry-on luggage. She tried to push it in front of her and then decided that pulling it was easier. A man stood up and helped her to readjust the bag on wheels. The red-headed woman next to him was looking out the window. Even though she had her back to Honey, she seemed familiar, somehow. Beautifully dressed with knee-length black boots that Honey thought she recognized. Quickly she moved forward to appease the impatient passengers caught in her luggage tangle.

By the time she reached her designated seat, she knew where she had seen those boots before. Becka had a pair. Just like them. But why did the lady seem so familiar? Honey was proud of her ability to recognize people. She remembered names and people's faces even after only one encounter. She had even remembered who David Knowles was when she heard that he had been burned to death a few days ago. Even though she was only twelve when Becka was dating him, she'd always thought David was really cute. She remembered how angry Becka was when he wouldn't go out with her anymore after their parents died. She wondered why she was thinking of that now. She figured it was because the red-headed woman reminded her of Becka. Silly really. She would see Becka as soon as she arrived in London. Hopefully Audrey had told her she was coming. Honey didn't really know Becka very well. Becka had left for London soon after Honey and Audrey had moved into Simone's little flat. They had corresponded at first, but eventually lost contact over the years. Honey was looking forward to spending some time with her. Getting to know her.

It was a ten-hour flight with a security-check stopover at

LAX. At least she could stretch her legs when they disembarked. She wondered how many of her fellow passengers were continuing on to London. She closed her eyes and tried not to think of the mess she was leaving behind. Thank goodness Audrey was taking care of everything.

CHAPTER
SEVENTY

The detective had called Eric Chapman numerous times and left many voice messages. Where the hell is he? He wanted to talk about Higgins' trip to Hihi. Had they met up that night? Had they both met with Audrey? Bromley left another message to contact him urgently and then opened up the Greta Baywater file.

A call to forensics revealed Greta had been poisoned. There was a list of toxins in her system: cardiac glycosides, saponins, digitoxigenin, oleandrin, oleondroside, and nerioside. When he had asked how the hell she'd ingested these toxins, the forensic pathologist advised that it was most likely she'd ingested the Oleander plant. It has been known to induce a heart attack and ultimately death.

"So she was poisoned?" he asked.

"Looks like it could have contributed to her death," he was told.

Did Deacon James have anything to do with it, he wondered. Bromley had read Greta's notes on Steve James and, as Audrey had suggested, James certainly had his reasons for keeping his sessions with Greta confidential. Being gay was not a motive for murder, but as the local deacon, married to the only daughter of one of the most affluent and prestigious families in the city, having a gay lover would destroy his reputation completely.

Bromley's call to Deacon James was not received well. At first he spoke to James' lovely wife, Naomi, who explained that her husband was at the church. It took some convincing for her to give Bromley his cell phone number.

"Why do you want to speak to Steve?" she asked. "What is it concerning?" She sounded annoyed, hostile even. When Steve James answered his cell phone, he was distant and not forthcoming with information. He said he had heard the news about Greta blackmailing church members and was calling a church meeting to discuss the matter with his parishioners that evening. Upon Detective Bromley suggesting that he might attend the meeting, Deacon James was adamant he should not do so. Furthermore, he stated that he had burned the notebook. "I didn't want to risk the information falling into anyone else's hands," he said. "I was shocked to hear Audrey Wetherby mentioned it at all." He agreed to meet the detective at the Whangarei Police Station at ten the following morning. Bromley didn't mention he was reopening the case due to new evidence. He didn't want to put James on the defensive.

It was a complicated case. One he had inherited from Higgins. Things were getting out of hand – this was all Higgins' mess. And now that Higgins was dead, Bromley had to clear up his mess.

All afternoon he had been in meetings with his superiors. He had been given a warning about not sharing information in a timely manner. *Well fuck them.* He had too much on his plate as it was. They had promised to give him a team from Kerikeri to assist. About time, too.

He made a note in Greta's file to have the team check out her neighbors. They may have seen someone coming and going on the day she and Ben died. His mind went back to who was there that day – Audrey Wetherby. But what would she have to gain from Greta's death? Even if Greta had information concerning Ben murdering his parents, it would not be a motive. After all, Audrey had gone to the media herself to spill her guts. No, he was missing something.

CHAPTER
SEVENTY-ONE

Deacon Steve James sat quietly waiting for the members of his church to take their seats. There was a sense of fear and uncertainty in the room. Looking at their faces, he knew everyone had heard the news that Greta Baywater had been exposed for blackmailing members of her church during fortune-telling sessions. Of course, they'd already known this, but hearing it on the nightly news was devastating. Their loved ones might think they were involved.

"There is no need for concern," Deacon James began. "As you know, we have burned the notebook. All record of our conversations with Greta has been destroyed. You have nothing to fear. I am meeting with Detective Bromley who is handling the case tomorrow morning. I will tell him the situation has been taken care of."

"Where has she stashed all the money she took from us? Surely we can claim it back. It was blackmail, after all," said a parishioner.

"Yes," others agreed.

"Then you will have to prove how much you gave Greta,

and, with the notebook destroyed, you will not be able to claim compensation." James responded.

"I want my money back. I don't care about what she might have written."

"Me too."

Deacon James was getting more and more frustrated. "Let's wait until I meet with the detective tomorrow."

The meeting was over soon after it had begun. The small crowd of disgruntled churchgoers shuffled out into the night, leaving Deacon James alone and distressed. He dialed a number.

"Craig, it's me. It looks like it isn't over yet. I am meeting with the police tomorrow morning. I don't know if I can take it anymore." He listened to his lover's soothing voice. "Alright, I'll come over on the way home. See you soon."

He hung up the phone, turned out the lights and locked the church. He knew he couldn't go on like this. If anyone found out, he would lose everything. He had a feeling the detective knew he had something to hide. It was a bad situation.

CHAPTER
SEVENTY-TWO

"We will be landing at LAX in twenty-five minutes. Please make sure your seat belts are fastened and your tray tables are returned to their original closed position. Please bring your seat upright and if you have footrests, please return them to their original position. We will be at the gate shortly. Thank you for flying with Air New Zealand. It has been a pleasure serving you. For those passengers continuing on to Heathrow airport, you will be required to collect your luggage and go through security before returning to the aircraft. Please take your hand luggage and boarding passes with you."

What a pain. Honey's bag was so bloody heavy. Maybe she could ask the nice man sitting next to the redhead if he would give her a hand. She hoped he was going through to London. It took ages for the passengers to disembark. There was a transit area for those passengers continuing on and she followed the crowd down the escalators. She saw the redhead walking with the man who'd helped her when she had boarded the aircraft.

They were ahead of her. She did look so familiar. It was the way she walked and held herself.

Much more confidently than Honey did. Honey always felt a little uncomfortable in a crowd. She walked faster, hoping she could catch up with them. As she was about to approach them, the woman headed into the ladies' bathroom. Honey made a choice. Dragging her carry-on, Honey followed her.

The woman had gone into a cubicle. Honey waited. In a few minutes the woman re-appeared. Bright red hair, huge sunglasses and flowing silk scarf reflected for an instant in the mirror then suddenly disappeared before Honey could even blink. *What! Shit! Was it… was it Becka? No. It can't have been. Becka's been in London for days. Shit, she looked so much like her. Could be her double. I must find her. Ask her if she lives in London. Wow. That was amazing!!!!!* Honey dragged her bag out into the passageway and headed towards security. Becka had a plain brown straight hairstyle. This woman's hair was bright copper with a mass of curls. What was she thinking? She laughed.

When she boarded the plane for Heathrow, the woman wasn't in her seat. Once the captain turned off the seat belt sign, she would sneak up to business class and see if the woman had returned to her seat. She just couldn't get her out of her mind. Maybe she had boarded late.

Honey hoped Becka would be waiting for her at Heathrow airport. If not, she had Becka's address. It was getting exciting. She was on an adventure. It was the right decision to leave New Zealand. Matt would be joining her in a few days. They could explore London together.

CHAPTER
SEVENTY-THREE

Detective Bromley looked down at the body of Eric Chapman. Inspector Burt was already at the scene along with the forensics team.

"Overdose my arse," said the inspector. "Too convenient if you ask me. First Higgins' body is found in Hihi Bay and now the private investigator working on his case is found dead in his home days later. If it smells bad – it is bad."

"What do we know, so far?" asked Bromley "We know that he was staying at the Hihi Motor Camp. He had been seen eating lunch with a red-headed lady in her forties. He hired a boat from Mangonui and apparently took the lady out for an afternoon on the bay. After that we lost trace of him. The motor camp people said he had not slept in his cabin last night. His Jeep is in the garage. He had unpacked so must have been here a while before his death occurred. It's not a robbery. It doesn't look as if anything was taken."

"Do we have a time of death?"

"Looks like about thirty-six hours ago. I will have more of an idea when I carry out the autopsy," said the Coroner.

"So that makes it late Thursday night. Is anyone talking to the neighbors? Maybe someone saw or heard him return?" Bromley asked.

"Yes, I have some guys on it now," replied the Super.

Bromley walked outside to a crowd forming around Chapman's front gate.

"I heard him return home in the wee hours of Friday morning," said a woman. "I am his next-door neighbor. I always wake at about three in the morning. Drives me crazy. I heard his car and looked out the window. It was he alright. He parked in the garage. The lights were on until about six."

"Did you see anyone else?" Bromley asked the woman.

"I saw a jogger. A girl. She was running down our street at about six o'clock. No-one else. Our neighborhood is pretty quiet," she explained.

"Do you suppose the girl had been visiting Mr. Chapman?"

"Could have been. He was quite a ladies' man, was Mr. Chapman. But I couldn't be sure."

Bromley thanked the woman and returned to the station. He had a meeting with Deacon James at ten. He was running late. He knew James would be annoyed at having to come to the station on a Saturday morning.

CHAPTER
SEVENTY-FOUR

ecka had seen her. Just for an instant her heart stopped. What was she doing in the LAX ladies' toilet? She was sure Honey hadn't recognized her. Her instincts were quick and effective. She disappeared in a second. She didn't board the plane until all the passengers had boarded. She was sure Honey would be sitting way back in coach. Becka was close to the front door of the plane. She knew she could disembark when they reached Heathrow long before Honey could make her way to the front of the plane. Her luggage was also marked "premier" which meant it would come off the belt first. Security would be the only problem. But she had dual passports. Carrying a UK passport meant she would be in a different security lane from Honey.

She figured Honey was coming to England to visit her. Fuck! What shitty timing. She needed to get home, dye her hair and give the impression she had been back for over a week. It wasn't going to be easy. Becka couldn't sleep. She couldn't afford to. What if Honey came wandering up into business class looking for her?

There was an empty seat on the other side of the plane. She grabbed her blanket and took the new seat. She was grateful for her black hoodie in her carry-on. She put it on, wrapped a blanket around her, put on her eye mask and settled in for the eleven-hour flight to Heathrow. *Shit! I bet this was Audrey's idea!*

"Would you like a drink?" the flight attendant asked politely.

"Maybe later." Becka was not in a drinking mood. She felt trapped. If Honey found out she'd still been in New Zealand till the previous day, she would tell Audrey and Simone. Before long the police would know and with her red hair it wouldn't take long for someone to figure out that she was the woman who'd been in Hihi with Eric Chapman.

Then she saw her. It was Honey. She was walking up the aisle on the other side of the plane. She stopped at Becka's empty seat. Becka held her breath as Honey looked around the business section.

"Can I help you?" asked a flight attendant.

"I was just looking for someone," Honey replied.

"I am sorry but this section is only for business class passengers. I must ask you to return to your seat," the attendant replied curtly.

"I'm sorry. But I thought I saw my sister. Becka Simpson?" Honey explained.

"I cannot give out names of our passengers. Please, I must ask you to return to your seat."

Becka watched as Honey turned and walked back to the coach section.

CHAPTER
SEVENTY-FIVE

I t was all over the news. Audrey stood and watched the mid-day report on her 56" flat-screen TV.

"Private Investigator, Eric Chapman, was found dead at his home on the North Shore at ten o'clock this morning. The police are treating his death as a possible homicide. It was Mr. Chapman who found Detective Constable Higgins' body only last Tuesday in Hihi Bay where they were reported to be on a fishing trip. We will keep you updated as new information comes to hand."

This is getting weird, she thought as she collapsed onto her huge chaise chair. Who is doing this? First Detective Higgins and now Chapman. Both were working on her parents' murder investigation. Both murdered. Shit! Was someone trying to frame her? Where was she when he was murdered? Was it yesterday? The day before? She had an alibi. She was working here at Tiromoana. After all, he was killed at his home in Auckland. Four hours' drive away from Hihi. The police would still think she could have driven there and back during the night. Shit! What was happening? *I'm just paranoid, she thought. Why would anyone suspect me? I had nothing to gain from their deaths. But who did?*

Audrey realized she couldn't just sit back and wait for the police to investigate her. She needed to find out who was responsible. She looked at the time. Honey would be arriving in London at ten thirty tonight. She would call Becka and make sure she arrived OK.

Traffic was coming up the driveway. Raised voices, car doors slamming. Who could that be? She pulled herself out of the chaise chair, checked her appearance in the full-length mirror and went to see what was causing the commotion.

Bright lights, cameras and reporters filled the car park and swarmed down the path. She took a deep breath and smiled. It was the beginning of what was to come. Audrey faced the crowd and quietly answered their questions. When asked if she knew why Detective Higgins and Eric Chapman might have been murdered and whether she thought it had anything to do with her parents' case, she could only shake her head and say she had no idea. And that was the truth, after all.

CHAPTER
SEVENTY-SIX

David Doherty couldn't believe his good fortune. His interview with Audrey Wetherby had proved to be the major scoop of his career. The thirty-year-old double murder of the Brown couple in Christchurch was the biggest unsolved murder in New Zealand history. He had downloaded all the old newspaper articles, interviews and reports he could find online. TV One had agreed to fund a full one-hour documentary on the case.

Over the past couple of days he been interviewing anyone and everyone associated with the case. He had even managed to get a quick interview with the private investigator, Eric Chapman, over coffee in Mangonui last Thursday. Chapman had been devastated by the recent death of his long-time friend, Detective Higgins. He had told Doherty they were both working on the Brown case when he died. Chapman was sure Higgins' death was a homicide. Later in the day, Doherty had been strolling along the Mangonui wharf and had noticed Chapman and a red-headed lady pulling into the dock in a snazzy-looking boat. He recognized her from the café. She had been sitting at the next table to them. He chuckled.

Lucky devil, he thought. He quickly shot off a few photos.

He had gotten the call just before noon. They had sent a camera crew to Chapman's home and interviewed Detective Bromley as he was leaving the scene. Shocking! The Detective thought Chapman died late on Thursday night or early on Friday morning.

Doherty told the detective he had met Chapman for coffee in Mangonui around lunchtime on Thursday and he also told the policeman about the redhead he had seen with Chapman later that afternoon. He had her photo. The detective asked him to email the photo to him. Maybe she had something to do with his death.

The story was getting bigger by the day. He had looked into the death of Ben Brown's caregiver, Greta Baywater, and discovered that her death was now also considered a homicide. Poison, the detective had told him. Possibly Oleander poisoning. Where had he seen a case like that before? He remembered. It was an old case from a couple of years ago. A lady. She was the sister of a guy who had murdered the poor girl in Hihi. Suicide, they said. Killed herself out of shame for what her brother had done. He had dumped the girl's body in Hihi bay. Was that a co-incidence? What did all these murders have in common? When he could find the common link, he would have the answer.

He opened the photos of the redhead on his laptop. She was a good-looking woman. In her forties he guessed. He emailed them to Detective Bromley. He had tried to do a photo search on Google but was unsuccessful. He hoped the police would have more luck.

CHAPTER
SEVENTY-SEVEN

etective Bromley sat looking at the photos of the redhead on his screen. Although the photos showed only a side view of the woman who was wearing huge sunglasses, he knew he had seen that face before; but where? She looked so familiar. Entering the photo in their database produced no result. She was an enigma. He pulled all the recent photos from the past couple of weeks. Photos from Greta Baywater's funeral, Ben Brown's funeral, Steve Brown's funeral. He searched through the faces and then he saw her. He knew who it was. It was Becka, Audrey's sister from London. Only she had different hair. This new woman had bright copper-red, curly hair. But he was sure it was the same woman. He sent off both sets of photos to forensics. They had computer imaging, facial-recognition software. Maybe they can confirm the photos are of the same person.

He picked up the phone and called Audrey. She didn't answer. He left a message. "Audrey, Detective Bromley here. Just wondering if you have managed to get hold of your sister, Becka. She has not returned my phone calls and I need to talk to her about signing a statement confirming your parents' death. Can you call me as soon as you get this message? Thanks."

Had Becka really returned to London? Was she still in New Zealand? He left another message on Becka's cell phone. Why had she had not returned his phone calls or responded to his emails. Where was she?

If this woman was with Eric Chapman on Thursday, then she would have possibly been the last person to see him alive. If he hadn't slept in his motel room on Thursday night, then there was a strong possibility he had been with this woman. His car was seen returning to his home in North Shore at two in the morning. Was this woman with him?

It was time for a meeting with the team.

First on the agenda. Call Air New Zealand and check if Rebecca Simpson was on a flight to London at any time during the past ten days.

Research any cases relating to Oleander poisoning in the past few years.

Set up interviews with relatives and friends of Eric Chapman. Was he in a relationship? Did he have any enemies?

Find a common link between all the recent homicides and compile a 'persons of interest' chart.

Arrange a press meeting for tomorrow. The media had been hounding him for an interview. Best to deal with it. By the time the meeting was bought to a close, Bromley was exhausted. He checked his phone. There was a message from Audrey. "I'm home. Call me."

CHAPTER
SEVENTY-EIGHT

"Yes, she left for London last Friday – over a week ago. Why?" Audrey asked the detective. "Yes, I have spoken to her. I talked to her before Honey and I gave our statements to you. We wanted to make sure she was supportive of our decision to talk to you."

"Was she calling from London?" he asked.

"I presume so. She called on my home line. I don't have caller ID on that phone," Audrey said. "Why are you asking?"

"Because we have reason to believe your sister is still in New Zealand. If you are at your computer, I would like to send you a photo."

"Yes, send it through." Audrey waited for her mail message to beep. "I am opening it now," she said.

"Is that your sister, Becka?"

Audrey looked at the beautiful redheaded woman on the screen. Her heart stopped. Her mind froze. Was that Becka? It looked like Becka. But her hair... what had she done to her hair? Then she saw the yellow dress and hat. Shit! "I don't know what to say, detective. It looks a little like Becka, but she is in London. It can't possibly be her. Where did you get this photo?"

"It was taken in Mangonui on Thursday afternoon. Are you sure she is in London? Have you talked to her in London recently?

"Of course she returned to London. And, yes. I talked to her about giving evidence about our parents' murders."

"When was that?"

"Maybe a week ago? I haven't seen her since."

What about your other sister, Honey. Has she talked to Becka?

"Honey left for London yesterday to stay with Becka. I bought her a ticket and she caught the 10.30 flight last night. I thought it better that she should be away from all the media craziness."

"When is she arriving in London?" Bromley asked.

"She should be at Becka's at about midnight tonight. I was going to call her."

"I would appreciate it if you could have Becka call me. She has not returned any of my messages and it is imperative I have a word with her."

"I will. Can you tell me why you are looking for her?" Audrey asked.

"If she is the woman in the photo then she may have been the last person to see Eric Chapman alive."

"Eric Chapman? You think she was with Eric Chapman?" Audrey was horrified.

"This woman and Chapman spent the afternoon together. Went out boating I understand."

"It can't be Becka," Audrey said. "You must be confused. She has never met Eric Chapman. You have made a mistake, detective. You have it all wrong."

"Just get her to call me," he said, and hung up.

Audrey sat looking at the woman on the screen and suddenly everything began to make sense. If it was indeed Becka then that would explain how Detective Higgins came to be floating in her bay. It explained how Eric Chapman ended up dead in his home. Was Becka a murderer too? If so, she was in deep shit.

There was one way to find out. Audrey walked over to her closet and searched for her favorite yellow dress. It was gone. Her floppy yellow hat was also missing.

CHAPTER
SEVENTY-NINE

oney stood on the curb outside Heathrow airport wrapped in her long black winter coat waiting in line for a taxi. Becka had not been there to meet her. She had waited for over half an hour before realizing she had been stood up. Damn. The trip was long and she was tired. It had taken forever to get through customs. She knew she should take the underground to Becka's house. It would be a lot faster, but dragging her heavy suitcase on and off the train would be just too much. Instead she decided to splurge on a taxi.

She had never been to Becka's house. In fact, she had never even seen a photo of it. But there it was. A three-storied, semi-detached brick house. All the houses looked identical along the street. They were separated by only a small pathway and tiny garden. So different from the brightly colored, eclectic houses in New Zealand.

She could hear music inside as she reached the front door. The taxi driver had been kind enough to drag her suitcases to the small porch. She knocked and listened.

Becka burst open the door. She was in her dressing gown and a towel was wrapped around her head. "I'm so sorry, Honey. I got home just half an hour ago and got Audrey's message to say you were coming. I have been in the country visiting a friend. Took a few days off to get away from things. Come in. Don't just stand there. I'm so happy you are here."

"I was worried when you didn't show at the airport," said Honey, following her sister inside.

"Just leave all your bags in the hallway. You will be sleeping upstairs on the third floor. We'll drag your bags up later. Come in and have a cup of tea. You must be exhausted."

"So you don't know that our parents' murder is all over the news in New Zealand?" Honey asked.

"Well yes, it is all over social media. Thank God we are over here and away from it all. How is Audrey handling it?" Becka asked as she turned on the kettle and grabbed a couple of cups.

The phone rang in the kitchen and Becka picked it up. It was Audrey. "Yes, hi Audrey. Honey is here. She just arrived. I have been out of town and just got your message. She is great. Do you want to talk to her?" She handed Honey the phone.

"Hi, Audrey. Yes, I just arrived. Yes, everything is fine. Becka? What do you mean? Of course she is just the same. OK. I'll tell her. Yep. Talk later. Bye."

"What was all that about?" Becka asked, "Oh she wants you to call Detective Bromley. Something about you having to provide a written statement or something." She sighed. "My god, it is good to be here. I think I will sleep for a week." Honey kicked off her shoes and sipped her tea. "Thanks Becka. Thanks for letting me stay."

"You're welcome," said Becka, removing her towel and shaking out her wet brown hair. "It will be nice to have some company."

CHAPTER
EIGHTY

Detective Bromley looked at the new text message on his phone. It was late, after midnight. The message was from Audrey. *Becka is in London. Talked to her and Honey. Honey says she looks just the same. I guess it isn't Becka in the photos. Told Becka you want to talk to her.* Bromley was surprised. He had asked his guys to get the Auckland airport surveillance tapes showing passengers boarding flights to London since Chapman's murder. Now he wondered if this was just a waste of time. If the woman wasn't Rebecca Simpson, who was she? He checked Audrey and Honey's statements. That was the name they had given him. Her married name. Had she changed her name since she divorced? He made a note to check.

The next morning he was at the Whangarei police station by seven thirty. Having tossed and turned all night, he was in a foul mood. His meeting was set for eight. He needed answers, now!

He learned there was no record of a Rebecca Simpson on any flight to or from London. "She didn't fly by stork!" bellowed Bromley. "Check if she is using another name."

Detective Bromley was familiar with Oleander poisoning due to a case he'd investigated a few years previously. A friend of his young daughter was found dead in Doubtless Bay, not far from where Higgins' body was found. The killer was later found shot by his own gun in Hihi.

Then the killer's sister was found, poisoned by the Oleander plant. It was considered a suicide.

And now Greta Baywater had supposedly taken her life by ingesting the same poisonous plant. A coincidence? They couldn't find any other case of the plant causing death, at least not in New Zealand.

The team reported they had managed to talk to the family of Eric Chapman and they had no knowledge of anyone who would want to harm him. However, his profession as a private investigator may well have caused him to have enemies. They were still working on his previous jobs and contacting his clients.

Detective Bromley put a list of names, location and cause of death on the board:

Ben Brown – Whangarei – brain cancer
Greta Baywater – Whangarei – poison leading to heart attack; suicide?
Steve Brown – Hihi – Alcohol/natural death
Detective Higgins – Hihi/Doubtless Bay – injury to head while fishing; murder?
Eric Chapman – North Shore – drug overdose or Murder?

What did they all have in common? What was the common link?

The first item he added was: Murray and Sophie Brown – thirty-year-old, unsolved murder case. "Every one of them was involved in the Brown case in some way," said Bromley. "Who else?"

The team looked at him in silence. "Who else? You are detectives. Do your job. Detect!" he hollered.

"Detective Higgins until he died," offered one of the team.

"Obviously the police," said Bromley. "As for who else, I want a list of everyone who came in contact or had any association with the victims, near or around the time of their deaths. I want it on my desk by five tonight."

The press conference was held at ten. Bromley didn't have anything new to add. "We are working on a number of leads," he told the reporters. "If anyone has any information surrounding the deaths of Detective Higgins and Eric Chapman, we hope they will come forward. These are tragic deaths."

A reporter asked, "Are their deaths tied up with the new evidence released by Audrey Wetherby in the death of her parents? We understand they were both working on this cold case before their deaths?"

"At this time, we have no proof that their deaths are as a result of their enquiries into this case. However, we are looking at all leads at this time. Thank you," he added as he stepped away.

A reporter called out, "What about Greta Baywater's death? Was her death also related to the Brown murders?"

"We have no proof of that," said Bromley. "At this time we are still considering her death to be a suicide."

CHAPTER
EIGHTY-ONE

Deacon James was glad the media were concentrating on the Brown murders rather than the death of Greta Baywater. He was online checking all the latest updates. His meeting with Detective Bromley was postponed until today due to the death of Eric Chapman. He was not looking forward to talking to the police. His life was his own business. He would not be divulging any personal information at the meeting. *No comment* would be his stance on the situation.

He looked around the sparsely furnished room. Small. Just a desk, two chairs and a two-way mirror. At least he figured that was what it was. He looked up as Detective Bromley and a policewoman entered the room.

"Thanks for meeting with us today," Bromley began. "This is Constable Johnston," he introduced his colleague. "Some information has come to our attention concerning Greta Baywater and we are hoping you could verify some the details that have come to light."

"I am happy to help in any way I can," Deacon James replied.

"We have a copy of Greta's notebook and from the contents we understand you had a number of meetings with her?" Bromley was asking for a confirmation.

James felt as if he'd been hit with a hammer in the chest. He couldn't breathe. *They had a copy of the notebook? Damn!* "I'm sorry Detective, I don't know what you want me to say. Yes, I did meet with Greta on a number of occasions. She was an avid churchgoer and a member of our congregation."

"That is not what I am referring to," Bromley explained. He was looking at the photocopied pages of the notebook. He read, '*Deacon James feels guilt but no remorse for this relationship with Craig. He says he loves him but cannot leave his wife, Naomi. He fears financial and personal ruin. He will pay me to keep quiet.*' Did you pay her?" the detective asked.

James was cornered. "I hope this conversation this stays in this room?" he asked.

"I can't make any promises. But if you come clean with us and had nothing to do with her death, then I can't see any reason why it should become public knowledge," he said.

"I love my wife," James offered. "I would never hurt her."

"Was Greta blackmailing you? Did you pay her to keep quiet?"

"Yes," his voice was hardly detectible, "I did."

"Did you kill Greta Baywater?"

"Of course not! I thought she committed suicide. Didn't she?" James was shocked at the accusation.

"Her death is still under investigation," Bromley replied. "Do you know if others from your church also paid her money?"

"Yes. There are others."

"I would like to take a statement from you including a list of all the members of the church you know were being black-mailed by Greta." Looking intently at James, he asked, "Can you tell me what you were doing between seven p.m. and midnight on the day of Greta's death?"

James knew exactly where he had been at the time. He remembered hearing about Greta's death the following day. His wife was out of town that night. He had spent all night with Craig. The last thing he wanted was to involve his lover in this sordid mess. He looked at the detective. "I was working late at the church. I was preparing for the Sunday sermon."

"I see," said the detective "And I presume you were alone?"

"I was, detective. I'm sorry I can't be of more help."

CHAPTER
EIGHTY-TWO

"Detective Bromley, Becka Simpson here. I understand you wanted to talk to me?"

"Yes, Becka. Thanks for getting back to me. I have a few questions. I understand you left for London the Friday before last, is that correct?"

"Yes. I have been back in London for over a week, Detective. Why?"

"Nothing important. I would like you to confirm some information your sisters have given us regarding your brother, Ben's, involvement in your parents' deaths. Do you have a moment?"

Becka confirmed everything her sisters had told the detective. "There is nothing more I can add. It was an awful time. I left for London and put all of that behind me," she added.

"Do you still have your boarding pass from your return flight to London?" he asked.

"Oh, I doubt it. I would have thrown it away by now," she replied. "Why do your ask?"

"Oh, just cleaning up some loose ends."

The phone call worried Becka. His questions regarding her return to London indicated that he doubted that she had been in London. Did he have some information that caused him to doubt that she had left New Zealand? Thank goodness she had changed her appearance. He might have his suspicions, but he obviously didn't have any proof or he would have accused her outright.

Becka's New Zealand trip had gotten a little out of hand. Killing the detective, the private investigator and the Knowles couple might come back to haunt her.

If this Detective Bromley got too close to the truth she might have to plan a return trip to Northland. She heard Honey coming down the stairs.

"Becka, I heard you on the phone, was that Audrey?"

"No, I was talking to Detective Bromley. He was just confirming what you and Audrey had already told him."

"Oh. Hopefully that is the last of that." Honey plonked herself down on the wide leather chair in the front room. "Thank goodness we are away from all the media frenzy. It must be driving Audrey crazy."

CHAPTER
EIGHTY-THREE

Reporters surrounded Audrey. Every television network in the country had interviewed her. It was also all over the news in Australia. It seemed they couldn't get enough. She had been approached to participate in a documentary about her parents' murder and her brother's involvement. They had offered her a pretty nice fee and it was tempting. As long as she could manipulate the facts to suit her own needs, she would continue to be interviewed. But the sooner this was all over, the better. Too many murders and too many loose ends.

Handing over her mother's diary and a copy of Greta's diary was a sound move. However, now that Detective Bromley had all the files on her parents' murder, it wouldn't take long before he came knocking at her door and asking more questions. And, speaking of the devil, she saw his car coming up the driveway. Excusing herself from the media, she returned inside to her office to await the detective's next move.

"Audrey, I have some questions relating to the night you

had dinner with Eric Chapman. What time did you return from dinner?"

"I'm sorry, I don't really remember. It was before midnight. We ate at the Carrington restaurant. It was quite late."

"Did you see him the following day? One of your guests saw him walking down to your beach past their cabin. He said he thought Chapman had been at your office."

"Yes, he came by to say goodbye. He was leaving for Auckland and wanted to take a stroll along the beach back to the motor camp."

"Did he ask you about Detective Higgins?"

"No, I had no idea he knew Detective Higgins. I had met Eric fishing on my beach. We started talking and the tide came in. I suggested he return to the camp via my property. He asked me out a day or so later. He never mentioned he was a private investigator."

"And you never saw Detective Higgins that night?"

"No detective. I never saw him."

"I have been going through Higgins' notes on your parents' case. He made a note that there were three schoolbags in the hallway on the afternoon of your parents' deaths. A photo clearly shows them inside the front door, hanging on pegs, proving that all three of you had been in the home that afternoon. Furthermore the photos from your father's collection confirm your stories of your parent's behavior towards you and your sisters."

The detective closed up his notebook and looked up at Audrey. "Higgins' notes also mentioned pearls. Your mother's pearls. Do you know anything about these pearls?"

"Yes, I have her pearls."

"How long have you had the pearls?" he asked.

"My brother had them. He gave them to me before he died," she lied.

"That would explain why you were wearing them the night your brother and his housekeeper died. Higgins made a note that you were wearing them when he interviewed you, immediately after their deaths."

"How did he know they were my mother's pearls?" she asked incredulously.

"Your mother was shown wearing them in a newspaper photo taken before her death. Higgins recognized them as the same pearls you were wearing the night your brother and Greta died."

"That was awfully observant. I wear them quite often." Audrey knew he had no proof she had taken them the night of her brother's death. Looking back she regretted wearing them that night.

"I don't suppose you would mind if I borrow the pearls for a day or two?" Detective Bromley asked.

"Why would you want to borrow them?"

"We are running DNA tests on a number of items and Higgins was quite sure your mother was wearing the pearls the night she died."

"I'll get them for you." Audrey removed them from her dresser drawer and handed them to the detective. "I would like them back."

"Of course. Thank you, Audrey. Oh, one last question. The night you found your brother and his housekeeper dead, did you see anyone else leaving the house, a car driving away? Anything?"

"No, I didn't see anyone. Do you think someone was in the house before I got there?"

"Greta Baywater was poisoned either by her own hand or by

someone else's." The detective looked intently at Audrey. "It seems she was poisoned by ingesting Oleander plant." He waited for her reaction.

"Oh, I thought her death was caused by a heart attack."

"Apparently brought on by the poison in her system."

"Do you think Deacon James might have something to do with her death?" Audrey asked.

"We have no proof. But he certainly had good reason to want her gone. But so did a number of members of his congregation."

Audrey was pleased when the detective took his leave. She poured herself a very large glass of Wither Hills Sav and took a well-deserved rest on her chaise chair.

She knew Deacon James had nothing to do with Greta's death but wanted to plant the thought in the detective's mind. She presumed he was already looking in James' direction. As for Detective Higgins' untimely death, she now knew that her sister, Becka, was responsible for that. But how? She obviously had not returned to London when she said she had. In fact, she was most likely responsible for her ex-boyfriend and his wife's deaths in Christchurch last week, too.

Why did Becka take her, Audrey's, yellow dress and hat? Why was she wearing the outfit the day she lunched in Mangonui with Eric Chapman? How did she meet him? Did she think she was doing Audrey a favor by killing him? Or was she framing Audrey?

And where was the dress now?

CHAPTER
EIGHTY-FOUR

Naomi James sat in deathly silence as her husband of fifteen years confessed his love for someone else. "I am so sorry," he kept repeating. "I'm so sorry. I never meant to hurt you. You have always been there for me. I am so sorry."

She waited to hear who it was. She knew she had married one of the best-looking men in the city. Women were constantly coming on to him but he had never looked at anyone but her. She had prided herself on keeping her figure, her looks. She was a woman of substance. A professional. Well-respected in her field. A partner in a prestigious law firm. She was born into a life of affluence. Both her parents came from wealthy backgrounds. They were constantly in the public eye. How would she explain this? How could he, after all these years?

She finally spoke. "Is it someone I know?"

"No, you have never met them." He couldn't say the word "he". He hoped she would never find out about Craig. "I think it's best if I stay in a hotel tonight. I have applied for the position of Deacon at the Dunedin Baptist Church and it looks as though I might be accepted."

"So you have it all planned. You're running away. You are a coward, Steve. Running away won't solve anything. How do you think you will survive without the luxuries you have become accustomed to? Good luck living off a Deacon's wages."

Naomi left her husband sitting on the sofa sniffling like a lost dog. Bloody men! She had spent the best years of her life with this man. Admittedly, he wasn't much in bed but he looked good on her arm. She had liked his calm manner and natural humility. These were two qualities she lacked. Tomorrow she would ask her partner to handle their divorce. No use stringing it on. She expected the divorce would cost her plenty. She earned four times his salary.

She went into her office and opened up the case she was working on. Naomi often worked into the wee hours of the morning. Half an hour later she heard the door lock and his car drive away.

CHAPTER
EIGHTY-FIVE

Deacon Steve James called Craig the moment he arrived at the Madison Hotel. Finally he was free. No more lies. The phone rang and went to voice message. "Craig, it's me. I have left her. I am staying at our hotel, room 23. Call me as soon as you get this message."

He lay back on the bed and sighed. It would only be a matter of time before the police pressed him further about his association with Greta. He was an obvious suspect. He would leave Northland and move down south. A new beginning.

He tried Craig's number again. Still no answer. He left another message and poured himself a drink out of the hotel's mini-bar.

He remembered the first time he saw Craig. It was at one of his wife's office parties. Craig was the new, up-and-coming lawyer. Tall, lean, gorgeous – with masses of blonde curly hair. He was young; too young. Naomi introduced them. Steve James couldn't take his eyes off him all night. He had followed him out onto the balcony where Craig was leaning over the balcony smoking a cigarette. Steve hated smoking but this beautiful young man gave cigarettes a whole new meaning. He had watched him as he slowly exhaled, blowing smoke into the cool night air. For an instant Steve imagined he could feel his breath on his cheek.

"Want one?" he asked Steve, without turning around.

"I don't smoke," he had replied rather guiltily, having been caught staring at him.

"I don't either," he laughed turning to face Steve. "Well, I am giving up. But I hate this type of event."

"Me too," he replied.

When Craig had asked, "Are you here with anyone?" he had lied and said he wasn't.

That was the first lie of so many. Steve had also lied about the evening Greta died. He had gone around to talk to her in the early evening. He was tired of her constant threats of exposure. He had threatened her. They had shouted at each other. A neighbor was mowing his lawn across the street. Steve was sure the man had seen him come and leave. He wondered if Ben Brown was already dead at the time of his visit. Greta seemed perfectly fit and healthy when he left. He was surprised to learn that she died shortly afterwards. Had someone else called on her after he left?

He tried Craig's number one more time. Still no answer.

CHAPTER
EIGHTY-SIX

Audrey stopped by her letterbox on the way into town. A large package was stuffed into it. She sat in the car and tore open the parcel. Her yellow dress and floppy hat peered out from the torn tissue paper. There was also an envelope. It contained Eric Chapman's receipt from the Hihi Motor Camp, and a note.

Thanks for the loan, Audrey. I thought you wouldn't mind.
After all, they were used in a good cause.

She stared in disbelief at the collection of items in the envelope. She had known when she discovered her dress was missing that Becka had been the woman in the photo. How she got back to London before Honey arrived Audrey couldn't imagine. But she was there and Audrey was here. Why had Becka used her dress? Did she want to implicate her in the crime? Why the receipt? Proof she had been with Eric? Fuck! Now what?

Audrey knew the grocery shopping could wait. She returned immediately to Tiromoana and to an empty trash can in the back of her garden shed. She placed the items alongside Detective Higgins' wallet and Greta's purse and bus ticket to Auckland. Now she had everything she needed.

She heard a car pulling into her car park and returned to her office in anticipation of the arrival of another guest. The cabins had been busy. She wasn't expecting the last guest to check in until early evening. She looked at the time. It was two o'clock.

She was surprised when her visitor opened the office door. She was beautiful. Immaculate. Obviously a businesswoman. Dressed to kill in an expensive tailored suit and extraordinarily high heels that made Audrey cringe thinking of the pain she must be enduring to submit to such torture in the name of vanity.

"Can I help you?" Audrey asked.

"I understand you know my husband, Steve James?" the woman accused, as she tucked an escaped red curl into her strangled bun. A gesture not lost on Audrey.

Audrey paused for a moment, "Oh, you mean Deacon James," she said. "I can't say I actually know him. I met him only once."

"That is hard to believe," the woman scoffed. "I know he has been up here recently. I spoke to his assistant at the church. She said he was here shortly after your brother and that awful fortune-telling woman died. He came to pick up some sort of diary. I hear you took a copy of the diary and I would like to see it."

"What makes you think I have kept a copy?" Audrey asked. "And, if I did, why should I give it to you?"

The woman handed her a business card. "I am asking as my husband's lawyer. I have a right to know if any information in this so-called diary could implicate my husband in any way with her death."

Audrey looked at the card. "I'm sorry, I cannot help you. I have handed everything I have over to the police. You can ask them for a copy if you are so worried."

The woman was obviously pissed off. She turned on her heel and strutted out of her office. Audrey watched her get into her Mercedes and slam the door.

A few minutes later the woman returned to the office carrying a computer bag. "My bloody car won't start. Damn technology. I have called the AA but they said it will take about an hour to get a mechanic here. Can I hire one of your little cabins for an hour so I can do some work?"

Audrey smiled. "By all means. You are welcome to use the Kiwi Cabin. Here is the key." She handed the woman the key to the cabin furthest from the office and out of sight of the car park. "There is no charge."

Naomi James took the key without a thank you or a kind word and disappeared down the ridge towards the cabins.

Audrey wasted no time. She knew what she must do. Putting on her gardening gloves, she removed the items from the trash can in the shed and placed them in a large paper bag. She waited until she was sure Mrs. James was settled in the cabin and then made her way to the Mercedes. Thank God it was unlocked. Opening the passenger door, she stuffed the brown bag under the passenger's seat and out of sight, quietly closed the door and returned to her office.

A couple of hours later she watched Mrs. James pay the mechanic and follow him down the driveway.

CHAPTER
EIGHTY-SEVEN

Detective Bromley finally had some quiet time to read Greta's notes. He noticed that the pages were not in chronological order. In fact they were not in any particular order. He decided to scan the pages and then cut and paste them into order by name, date and time.

He began with Deacon James. There were so many entries. Some were just a line or two. Some were more detailed. He had visited her almost every Wednesday for over a year. Greta Baywater was a strange woman. She didn't appear to offer any opinions on what her clients were telling her, but instead just documented the facts. Detective Bromley guessed it was her way of collecting damaging information in order to blackmail them.

He looked at the lines of facts relating to Deacon James. They were revealing. There was no doubt the man was wracked with guilt. Ashamed of his homosexuality. As he neared the end of his session notes, Bromley gasped. Bloody hell! The man was there the night of Greta's death. It was there in Greta's own handwriting.

The deacon stopped by without an appointment tonight. He didn't want a reading. He was angry.

Threatened me. Said he would see me dead before he paid me any more money. I have to leave. My bags are packed. I have my ticket to Auckland.

Bromley took a deep breath and let it out slowly. It felt so good he did it again. All the pressure of the past few days had been overwhelming. His job, his reputation and his livelihood were on the line. For the first time he had some concrete evidence that Deacon James not only had a motive but also that he was there the night Greta Baywater died.

This time he would keep his Super in the loop. He would request a search warrant for Steve James' home, office and car. They would need to be careful. All the t's crossed and i's dotted. James' wife was an influential lawyer and she would be fighting them every step of the way.

He dialed the Super's number. This call he was looking forward to.

CHAPTER
EIGHTY-EIGHT

Naomi James was more than pissed off. She was livid. Bloody woman. I should have known she wouldn't give me the damn copies of the notebook. What was I thinking? It is not like me to act irrationally. I should never have driven there. Now the fucking car needs servicing. I will have to take it in tomorrow. Damn Steve. His timing couldn't be worse. I am up for a senior partnership at the firm. My bosses like a women to be free of family problems. They have no tolerance for divorce. "It shows weakness," they say. *Well, fuck them!*

As she passed the "Welcome to Whangarei" sign, her cell phone rang. She pushed the button on the console. "Naomi James," she spat into the phone. "I will be in the office in twenty minutes," she said, and hung up.

I can't even get away for a few hours without them checking on me. She had hoped that Audrey Wetherby would give her the information she desperately wanted – the name of the slut her husband was screwing.

As she drove into her office car park, she saw two detectives entering her building. She knew them. They often worked on cases together. She followed them in.

When they saw her they looked embarrassed.

"I'm sorry Naomi, but we wanted to give you the heads-up. We have a warrant to search your home, your husband's office and your vehicles. We cannot locate your husband and were hoping that you could tell us where he is?"

Naomi's professional world collapsed in that moment. Bringing her personal life into the office was a major no-no. Bringing scandal into the office would be sure to jeopardize her senior partnership.

She ushered the detectives into her office while her bosses stared in disbelief. They had heard every word. It would be all over the town now.

"I don't know where Steve is. He left last night and said he was staying in a hotel. You could try the Mayflower or the Madison on Main. Have you checked the church?"

"Yes, they say he has not been in today. If you hear from him, please ask him to contact us immediately."

"Can I ask what this is about?"

"Will you be acting as his lawyer?" the detective asked.

"Yes, but I will need to know why you are searching our home. What are you looking for?"

"At this time, your husband is a person of interest in the death of Greta Baywater. We cannot tell you anything more. Please have your husband come down to the police station. We need to ask him some questions."

"You have to be joking. There is no way Steve would commit a crime. He is a religious, kind man. Ask anyone." Naomi knew her husband might be a cheat and a liar, but a murderer he was not. He didn't have enough balls to kill anyone.

When the detectives left she grabbed her keys and told the receptionist she would be at home if anyone was looking for her.

CHAPTER
EIGHTY-NINE

Deacon James was beside himself with worry. Craig had not returned his calls. He must have called twenty times and left twenty messages. Nothing. What was worse, James could not go to his home and ask where he was. Craig was not only a new lawyer in his wife's firm, but he was also a parishioner's twenty-five-year-old son. James knew he had broken his marriage vows, committed adultery, performed homosexual acts and lied before his God. How could he possibly consider carrying on in God's work? He looked at the gun lying on the bed beside him. He held it in his hand. It was cold, unfamiliar, and heavy. He had never used a gun in his life. Could he use one now?

The phone on the bedside table rang. The piercing sound shook him to his core. He didn't want to talk to anyone. Then he felt a sudden rush of expectation. Putting down the gun he reached for the phone. It must be Craig. He'd told Craig where he was staying. Maybe he was downstairs. Then he realized it wouldn't be Craig. He would come to the room. He left the phone in its cradle, unanswered. He looked at his cell phone.

Nothing. Not even a call from Naomi. His hopes squashed. The phone went silent. He picked up the gun and opened the box of cartridges. The gun belonged to Naomi. She was a gun fanatic. He had watched her load it many times.

They were in the room before he had a chance to load the gun. "He's got a gun! Put your hands in the air," they shouted. He obeyed. They handcuffed him, took him downstairs and put him in a police car.

Sitting in an interview room, he waited. They had his cell phone. They would see all his text messages to Craig. He was screwed. They would know. Naomi would know. The whole congregation would know.

He looked up as Detective Bromley entered the room.

CHAPTER
NINETY

Waking up at the crack of dawn was something Audrey didn't do. At least not anymore. Her days of rushing to O'Hare airport at four in the morning had been replaced with a comfortable seven o'clock start at Tiromoana Cabins.

Today was different. She had agreed to be interviewed on the morning's *Breakfast Show* on TV One.

"So, Audrey, we understand the thirty-year-old case of your parents' murder has finally been solved. It must be dreadful for you to have it all resurface and your personal life be exposed so publicly?"

"We were just children at the time our parents were killed. We are just pleased it is now over and we can get on with our lives."

"I understand a movie is going to be made telling your story of the awful events?"

"Well, that is not decided yet. Right now I just want to live quietly, finally forget the past and look forward to the future."

"Your sisters must also be relieved the case is closed. You have three sisters?"

"Yes, they just ask to retain their anonymity. I have agreed to answer any questions on behalf of my siblings."

"So tell us about your brother. Were you a close family growing up?"

"Yes, prior to our parents' deaths, we were all pretty close. Although my brother and my older sister had left home by the time of the incident. As we became adults, we became estranged. The past was too horrific. It was not until our brother's death that we were reintroduced to one another's lives."

"You have said you were all abused by your parents and that your brother killed them to protect you. You knew about this but didn't tell the police until just a few days ago."

"The death of our brother and his caregiver opened up the case again. We couldn't keep the truth to ourselves any longer. It was time to close the case once and for all. Our brother was dead – he couldn't be hurt anymore."

"You mention your brother's caregiver. We heard this morning someone is being held for questioning in connection with her death."

"Is that right?" said Audrey. "No, I have not heard about that."

"We also have heard her body has been exhumed and that a toxicology test was performed. Do you think she was drugged or poisoned?"

"That is for the police to find out. I had presumed she died from the shock of finding my brother dead. They were very close, you know."

"But she was a fortune teller, a scammer and a blackmailer. Do you think it was one of her clients who killed her?"

"If the police have someone in for questioning, then maybe

it was. I have to say I was surprised to learn she was not the church-attending woman I thought she was."

"Well, we have run out of time. But we wish you all the best, Audrey."

"Thank you." Audrey was pleased it was over. She just hoped her interview would solidify the perception of her innocence and encourage the police to let sleeping dogs lie. After all, they had bigger fish to fry. Of course she had heard that Deacon James was brought into custody yesterday. She had talked to Detective Bromley before James was arrested. He had asked her if she had seen James at her brother's house when she arrived the night of Greta's death. Had she seen his car? Audrey was surprised to hear he had been there that night. *Had he seen her?*

She had confided in the detective that she had been visited by the Deacon's wife who wanted to see Greta's diary notes. Naomi James was apparently acting as her husband's attorney. The detective thought it strange she was representing her husband who hadn't, at that time, any reason to have legal representation. Did they both have something to hide? Did she know something he didn't know? He made a note to check they had done a thorough search of her home, office and vehicle.

CHAPTER
NINETY-ONE

Naomi James knew that Audrey Wetherby had something to do with her husband being taken in for questioning. Her visit to Audrey was a mistake and one she knew she would regret for a long time. Very seldom did Naomi let her emotions get the better of her. But the need to find out the name of her husband's lover was driving her crazy. As soon as she met Audrey, she didn't trust the woman. Of course Audrey had copies of Greta's client notes. A woman like that would not have handed everything to the police. It takes a schemer to know a schemer. And Audrey Wetherby was a schemer. Of that Naomi had no doubt.

All that business with her parents' deaths – blaming it all on her dead brother. Naomi knew there was more to the story than Audrey was telling. She called her PI friend and asked him to do a background search on Audrey. She wanted to know everything there was to know about her.

For hours the police searched their home and Steve's office at the church. Nothing. She knew they would find nothing. They had confiscated Steve's car at the hotel and taken it for forensic testing. What the hell they were looking for, she had no idea. Her car was in the workshop getting repaired. Something to do with the electrical system. It would not be ready until the end of the week. She was using a company car in the meantime, which they had also confiscated.

The police also took boxes of Steve's files and his computer away. Naomi wished she had found Steve's cell phone. She was sure the police would have it by now.

The house phone rang. It was a woman from Steve's church. She was looking for Steve. It was urgent. Naomi explained he was not there. Could she take a message? The woman sounded agitated. "No," she said. "Just tell him to call me as soon as he can. It is about Craig. He will know what I'm referring to."

"Craig?" She wondered if it was the same young Craig who worked at her firm. "Your name?" she asked.

The woman just left her phone number. "Please, it is urgent."

Naomi wrote down the phone number and put it in her pocket. She was due at the police station. They were questioning Steve and she wanted to be there. She would get him out of there. They had no evidence, nothing to hold him. She needed to clear his name quickly and repair any damage that had already been done, in order to try to salvage her career.

She called a cab.

CHAPTER
NINETY-TWO

Detective Bromley sat facing Deacon James across the desk in the small interrogation room. They were alone. Others were watching out of sight.

"We have evidence you visited Greta the night she died." Bromley got straight to the point. "What were you doing there?"

"I went to ask her to stop blackmailing me."

"Did you threaten her?"

"I told her that if she didn't stop she would be sorry."

"Did you see or hear Ben Brown while you were there?"

"No. He must have been sleeping."

"Or was he dead?"

"I have no idea. I didn't see him or hear him."

"So you and Greta had an argument. Can you tell me what she said when you threatened her?"

"She said she was leaving anyway. She had booked a ticket on the bus to Auckland. She was packing her suitcase."

"You saw her packing her suitcase?"

"Yes, I followed her into her bedroom. I was so mad when she walked away from me. I hadn't finished venting and I was surprised to see her packing everything she owned and putting it into an old red suitcase. She had emptied every drawer. They were left open and the wardrobe was empty. I remember thinking I didn't have to worry as she was leaving."

Bromley remembered the Oleander poisoning. "Was she making tea or preparing any drinks when you were there?"

"No, but I saw a big pot of water on the stove.

She had just turned the stove on when I arrived there. I guess she was making tea or something. I left her packing her suitcase in the bedroom and took off. She told me she was leaving for good and not coming back and I need not worry. She wouldn't contact me again."

"Did you believe her?"

"I didn't have much choice. It wasn't until later when I heard she had died that I worried she may have kept notes of our meetings. That is when I contacted her nephew and asked him to look for any notebook or diary."

"And her nephew found it and gave it to you?"

"Well, actually it wasn't her nephew. It was Audrey Wetherby. She found the notebook and handed it to me when I drove up to meet with her nephew. She said she had found it in her brother's possessions. She made me promise to burn it. And I did. I had no idea she had kept a copy."

The door opened and Naomi James entered the room. "Steve, you don't have to answer any questions. Detective Bromley, my client wishes to say nothing more." She looked at Steve. "Come on Steve, I am getting you out of here." She looked at the detective. "That is unless you have grounds to keep him here?" she asked.

"I could keep him here on a charge of possession of a firearm without a license," he said.

"Steve does not own a gun. I do and I have a license." She looked at her husband. "What were you doing with a gun?"

"I don't know. I wasn't planning on hurting anyone. Just myself," he replied.

"Take him," said the detective. "He is all yours. But don't go too far away. We will have more questions," he said to Steve as Naomi took his arm and led him out of the room.

"Why the bloody hell did you take my gun?" Naomi asked. "You certainly have screwed everything up."

"I didn't kill Greta," he said.

"Of course you didn't," said Naomi, "but you sure have made a mess of things."

Detective Bromley walked into his office, picked up the Deacon's cell phone and began to scan through the messages. What he read explained a lot. The good Deacon was having an affair with a guy named Craig. Now, that was a surprise. He bet the beautiful Naomi James had no idea. He dialed Craig's number and got a voice message. "Detective Bromley here, I would appreciate it if you would return my call." He left his number and sat back in his chair.

Somehow he couldn't imagine Deacon James poisoning Greta Baywater. And, furthermore, he had learned something that altered the course of the investigation; Greta had packed her suitcase and bought a ticket to Auckland. So why did the crime scene notes say her room was neat and tidy and there was an empty suitcase on top of the wardrobe? He had been perturbed by the awkward angle of the suitcase in such an immaculate room. It was as though someone else had put it there. Had someone unpacked her suitcase to make it look as though she was not leaving and then murdered her and made it look like suicide? But who would have done that? Who would want the old lady dead before she left town? And why had they not taken her notebook and destroyed it? Did her murder have nothing to do with black-mailing? Was it always about the Brown murders thirty years ago?

CHAPTER
NINETY-THREE

Matt Walters had promised Honey he would meet up with her in London. However, he just couldn't see himself leaving now that he'd heard the news his aunt had been poisoned and the police suspected foul play. He had called Honey to explain and the sweet woman said she was coming home on the next flight. He had missed her robust laugh and silly hats. As a surprise he had collected her cats from the cattery and taken them home to her place. He watered her plants, did some grocery shopping and headed off to the airport to meet her plane.

Honey looked a million dollars pushing her trolley overflowing with suitcases. He could see she had been shopping in London. He swept her up in his arms and she glowed with happiness. "You are such a dear coming to meet me. I missed you so much. It is so great to be back."

On the way back home, Matt filled her in on what had been going on. "It would appear that the emphasis has shifted from your parents' murders to my aunt's murder. Although they are not calling it murder, they now know she was poisoned and there was no trace of the poison in the house at the time of her death."

"That is awful! Do they suspect anyone?" she asked.

"I heard they took Deacon James in for questioning. There was some talk of him having a gun or something. But his wife, who is a lawyer, got him released. I will call Detective Bromley tomorrow and see if he has any further information. He is handling the case now that Higgins is dead."

Honey crashed on her sofa and hugged her cats.

"What have I done to deserve you?" She removed her new boots and flung off her coat. "It was so cold in London. I'm so happy I'm back."

"Was it nice getting to know Becka?"

"Funny you should ask that. Becka acts friendly but isn't. If you know what I mean? We have very little in common. I just wanted to tour the city, go shopping and see some shows. Becka seemed pre-occupied – restless. I think she was pleased to see me go."

"Well, I am happy you are back." Matt opened a bottle of her favorite wine and they sat talking until Honey said, "I'm starved. What do we have to eat?" He laughed. She was home. He doubted he would be going home to his house any time soon. How could he leave this wonderful, vibrant, sexy woman? "How about a shrimp stir-fry?" he suggested.

CHAPTER
NINETY-FOUR

Awkward would not even come close to describing the atmosphere in the James household. Steve James was shocked to see what the police had done to the house. Drawers open, papers everywhere. What the hell were they looking for? They had even removed the cushions from the sofa and the bedding from the beds. His computer was gone and they had taken his cell phone. All he could do was wait until he was exposed as a homosexual, "a poofter". It wasn't that New Zealand was homophobic, it wasn't, but his church was. And his wife would be horrified and shamed by it.

Naomi had not said much since they had returned home. She had insisted that he stay at home until everything got sorted out. He figured the embarrassment her husband's arrest caused her was enough to deal with without the added trauma of his extramarital affair.

He watched her methodically putting her office in order. Returning files, straightening up her desk. He felt sorry for her. He never meant to hurt her. She was not a warm woman. Most of her colleagues described her as cold and unapproachable, but she demanded very little of him either sexually and emotionally.

Naomi joined him in the lounge and poured them both a drink. "Oh, I forgot, a woman from your church called and wants you to call her." She handed him the phone number. "She said it was about Craig and you would know what she was referring to. The woman sounded quite frantic."

Steve couldn't hide his shock. Fuck! The whole church will know now. He put the note it in his pocket.

"I'll call her later," he said. "I can't deal with church business right now."

Naomi considered her husband's obvious distress. "You know you can tell me anything," she said. "You didn't have anything to do with Greta's death, did you Steve?"

"I can't believe you are asking me. Of course I didn't."

"Why did the police want to talk to you? You should have waited until I got there before answering any questions. I need to know if I am going to get you out of this."

"They just wanted to know whom Greta was blackmailing." How could he explain why he had gone to see Greta that night? "Look, Naomi, I just can't talk about it tonight. I need to get some sleep. I haven't slept in a couple of days. Can we talk about this tomorrow?" Tomorrow she would know everything. It was a small town. News travelled fast. He closed the door of the guest bedroom, sat on the bed and looked at the note. He had nothing to say to Craig's mother. He knew he couldn't go in to work tomorrow and face his congregation. Why hadn't Craig returned his calls? Now the police had his phone. He could see no way out of this. He was ruined.

CHAPTER
NINETY-FIVE

Detective Bromley had called his team together. He listened as they reported their findings from the past couple of days.

"We found a neighbor across the street from Ben Brown's home who said he saw a car pull out of that driveway about seven o'clock that evening," reported one of his team members. "He remembered because he thought it looked like Deacon James. He is a member of his church. But the man was driving a Mercedes, not his usual Ford Explorer. He said the man left in a hurry."

"Did he see him arrive?" asked Bromley.

"The constable looked at his notes. "He said the car had been there for about half an hour or so. He was mowing the lawns at the time and didn't see the man arrive, only saw him leave."

"I have spoken to a neighbor who thinks they saw a lady walking towards the Brown house just upon dusk. It was getting dark and she couldn't see who it was but she could tell it was a woman by the way she walked."

"She didn't come in a car?"

"No, she was on foot, apparently."

"Anyone else?" Bromley asked his team. No-one responded.

"I couldn't find any record of Ben's sister, Becka, traveling to or from London during the past couple of weeks," another team member advised.

"She can't have flown by stork!" Bromley was annoyed. "Keep on it! Anything else?"

"We have researched Oleander poisoning and it would appear that Greta Baywater could have consumed the plant in various forms. It is impossible to know when and how she had access to it. But we did find the plant in her garden. It is a common plant here in New Zealand."

Bromley wasn't getting anywhere. The information just confirmed what he already knew. "I need you to follow up on who the woman was who visited the Brown home after Deacon James. I have learned that Greta Baywater was packing to leave on a bus trip to Auckland and yet, when her body was found, there was no sign of a packed suitcase in the house. All her clothes had been returned to their original place. This indicates that someone either made her change her mind or they killed her and replaced the garments to make it look like she had not planned on leaving. This is a major game changer. We need to know who was with her the night of her death."

When the team dispersed, Bromley wondered why Deacon James was driving a Mercedes the night he visited Greta. He called his forensics team and asked if they had searched a Mercedes car belonging to the James family. He learned that no Mercedes was present on the property the day they did their search. "Find the Mercedes!" Bromley bellowed into the phone.

CHAPTER
NINETY-SIX

M ary Hastings' world was collapsing around her. Now she regretted going to police and handing over Greta's blackmailing notes. She heard that Greta had been poisoned and that Deacon James was taken in for questioning. News traveled fast in their church. Gossip was paramount in their close friendships. But this gossip was going to destroy her.

Yesterday, her son, Craig, confessed he had been having an affair with Deacon James. Her beautiful son, who had worked so hard to become the young lawyer she was so proud of. To make matters worse, he worked in the same firm as Deacon James' wife, Naomi. She had never really met Naomi. But heard she was as tough as nails; a cold woman.

Mary had always suspected her son was gay. It didn't really bother her but they never spoke about it. Her church was not forgiving when it came to homosexuality. She loved her son no matter what. But his confession of their affair was bought on by Deacon James' arrest yesterday. Craig realized his association with the Deacon could ruin his career. Would ruin his career.

Once Naomi James found out, it was likely that he would be fired. Craig was devastated. Mary had left a message for Deacon James to call her. She was still waiting for the call.

Mary hadn't told anyone she had gone to see Greta that night. She lived only a few houses from the Brown residence. She saw Deacon James' car parked in the driveway and she waited until he left. She walked around to the back door and found it open.

She wanted to have it out with Greta. Tell her to stop blackmailing her. She had no money. She was a single mother who had put her son through law school. She hoped that Greta would feel remorse for what she had done.

When she walked into the house, she saw a pot boiling on the stove. She walked down the dark corridor and found Greta packing clothes into a suitcase on the bed. Greta had turned to face her with a snarl on her face. "What brings you here?" she said as she continued folding clothes neatly into the case.

"We need to talk. This has to stop," Mary pleaded.

The talk did not go well. Greta told her to leave. "I will not be bothering you anymore," she said, slamming the lid of the suitcase shut. "I am leaving, going away. Get out of my house!"

Mary had seen a different side of Greta. No longer was she the sympathetic listener Mary used to tell her secrets to. Instead she was a mean, shriveled old woman who tormented her. Mary almost felt sorry for the old woman. Good riddance to her. As she left by the front door, she saw a woman walking around the side of the house towards the back door. She presumed it was one of Greta's clients.

Mary had taken her revenge by passing on Greta's blackmailing threats to the police. She wanted them to know how evil the woman was. Now she wished she hadn't got involved. She wondered if Deacon James had returned that night. If

Deacon James was guilty of killing Greta, her son would be implicated in the scandal.

Craig's cell phone rang. Thinking it was Deacon James, she answered.

"Detective Bromley here. I am looking for Craig Hastings."

"He is not here. Can I take a message?"

"Do you know where I can reach him?" he asked.

"Yes, he works at Bartlett, Broomfield and Dickenson, the law firm on Main.

"I see. Thank you." The phone went dead.

Damn! Craig left his phone at home so he wouldn't be hassled by the Deacon's constant calls. She had told him to leave it with her. She wanted to talk to Deacon James. Now she had really messed things up. She picked up her bible and sighed. It is in God's hands now.

CHAPTER
NINETY-SEVEN

Naomi James returned to her office the next morning. She wasn't one for avoiding trouble. She had made a career out of winning legal battles and she was ready to fight this one. No matter what. When Detective Bromley walked into their offices, she presumed he was coming to see her. He was surprised to hear him ask for Craig Hastings. What the hell would he be wanting with their new young lawyer? She watched as they went into their conference room and shut the door.

She wondered if he was the "Craig" the woman had referred to in the phone call. Did Craig know her husband? What was their association? Thirty minutes later the detective left and Craig picked up his briefcase and followed him out of the office.

Naomi called Steve at home. There was no reply.

Her office phone rang. "There is a detective here wanting the keys to your Mercedes. They said they have a warrant."

Fuck! Fuck! Fuck! Why won't they leave us alone? "You can

come in and get them," she said to the receptionist. "Ask them if I will have my car back by the end of the day."

Why would they want to search my car? What could they possibly expect to find in it?"

Naomi wondered if she was becoming a suspect in the murder of Greta. She remembered that night. She had told Steve she was going out of town. But it was a lie. She just wanted some time to herself. Her family owned a little seaside cottage half an hour out of the city. She had gone there and stayed until the following morning. She had no alibi. She had taken their four-wheel drive, as the country road was steep, and had left her Mercedes at home. Had Steve taken it that night? Is that why they were interested in it? Was he guilty after all?

She tried calling Steve again. Still no reply.

CHAPTER
NINETY-EIGHT

Deacon James finally received a return call from Detective Bromley.

"We released your friend Craig an hour ago," the detective advised. "He is not a person of interest in the death of Greta Baywater. We just wanted to confirm his whereabouts at the time of the crime. You will be pleased to know he said he was with you at the Madison Hotel from seven fifteen that evening until seven the next morning. The hotel has confirmed this. Furthermore," the detective added, "we have a witness who saw a woman entering Greta's house later in the evening. We are following up this lead."

James gave a sigh of relief. "Then it is over?" he asked.

"As far as you and Craig Hastings are concerned, it is over," the detective confirmed.

"So there is no need for anyone to know about our relationship?" James asked hopefully.

"You are both adults. What you do is your business. We certainly have no plans to divulge any information regarding your relationship."

"Thank you, Detective. That is good news." Deacon James felt a huge weight lift from his shoulders. "So I can pick up my cell phone and computer?"

"Yes, any time. Oh, there is just one more thing. Whose car is the Mercedes?"

"It is my wife's car. Well, actually her firm's car. Why do you ask?"

"It was not at your home at the time of the search."

"Oh, yes, my wife had to take it in for a service."

"I see. Thank you." The detective hung up.

Deacon James knew it was over with Craig. The fact that he had not returned any of his calls and that his mother was aware of their relationship pretty much said it all. Sooner or later his sexual preference would be a topic of conversation amongst his congregation. It was time for him to leave the church and find a new career.

He also knew his marriage to Naomi was over. He would move out tomorrow and file for divorce. No more secrets. No more lies.

Deacon James was packing when he heard the home phone ring. It was Naomi. "You set me up!" she screamed into the phone. "You bastard!" The phone went dead.

CHAPTER
NINETY-NINE

The arrest shocked the city of Whangarei. The six o'clock news captured the attention of Northland viewers. Audrey was no exception. She watched as Naomi James was lead away from her law office to a police car.

"Detective Bromley, the lead investigator has just released a statement," the announcer said, as the detective's familiar face appeared on the screen.

"We have made an arrest in the murders of Greta Baywater, Eric Chapman and Detective Higgins. Earlier today we found evidence that strongly implicates a local lawyer, Naomi James as the perpetrator of all three crimes.

"At this time we cannot go into details but we can say we expect this case to go to trial. Mrs. James has been remanded in police custody and her case will be heard in the Whangarei District court tomorrow when the judge will make a decision on whether she will be released on bail until her trial.

"The arrest of Mrs. Naomi James was the result of hard work on the part of our team of the Northland police force from Mangonui to Whangarei."

Deacon James' home was surrounded by reporters. As he walked outside to his car, carrying a suitcase, they converged on him.

"Deacon James, did your wife kill Greta Baywater because Greta was blackmailing you?"

"Why did she kill the detective and the private investigator? What are you hiding?"

"I have no comment," he said.

A pretty blonde reporter called out," Did you know your wife was a murderer, Deacon James?"

"No comment," was all he said.

Audrey's phone rang. It was Honey. "Did you hear? Shit!! It was the deacon's wife, Naomi, who murdered them all. I can't believe it, Audrey. I wonder what evidence they found? Wow!"

Audrey heard a man's voice in the background. "Is Matt there?" she asked.

Honey laughed. "Yep. Guess what Audrey? We are engaged! Matt and I are getting married!"

"Oh, Honey. Congratulations. I am so happy for you."

They said goodbye. Audrey wondered if they would stay in touch. Somehow she felt they would return to their separate lives. It was murder that separated them and murder that reunited them. A bond they were destined to share again.

Audrey did not expect to hear from Becka. She knew the evidence found in Naomi's car was a joint effort. Without Becka's help, she wouldn't have been able to frame Naomi for Greta's murder, too. Did Becka know she was responsible for Greta's death? Or was Becka only looking after her own interests? Protecting herself? Audrey would never know.

She made a call to Simone. She hadn't talked to her since Simone left Tiromoana. Simone sounded pleased now that the emphasis had shifted from their parents' death to Greta Baywater's death. As usual, she seemed somewhat uninterested in it all. "Did I tell you? Piper is going to spend next year in France on a foreign student exchange."

"That's wonderful, Simone. Give her my love." Audrey said goodbye.

It was time for a celebration. Audrey popped the cork of her favorite champagne, Tattinger Brut,

poured a glass and sat at her computer. She opened up Greta's bank account information. A quick transfer of $200,000 into her overseas account put a smile on her face. She poured herself a second glass of champagne and fondled her mother's pearls.

"To family," she toasted.

THE END

ALSO BY LEONIE MATEER

THE AUDREY MURDERS – BOOK SERIES

The Murder Suite —Book One

The Cabin by the Sea — Book Two

The Murder Trail — Book Three

Murder in the Family — Book Four

The Murder Trap — Book Five

Murder in Lockdown — Book Six

The Taupo Bay Killings — Book Seven

If you enjoyed this book, I would be so appreciative if you would write a brief review on Amazon. Thank you.

Leonie Mateer

www.leoniemateer.com

ABOUT THE AUTHOR

Puppeteer, children's entertainer, model agency owner, TV talk show panelist, luxury accommodation owner, entrepreneur, product developer, brand developer, storyteller, author, and indie publisher Leonie Mateer has lived a full and diverse life.

Born and raised in New Zealand, Mateer moved to the United States in her thirties to pursue business opportunities. She returned to New Zealand for several years in the 2000s, running a luxury lodge in Northland—which has been an inspiration for her crime series—and now splits her time between Northland, New Zealand, and the United States.

Mateer is known for her huge success as a brand development expert. She received 'Who's Who' awards from both Leading American Executives and American Inventors in the 1990s. As the creator of the brand Caboodles™, a teen girl brand that took the retail industry by storm in the late 1980s and early 1990s, she created a new retail category—the cosmetics organizer category—with Caboodles' global retail sales exceeding US$100 million worldwide.

Ms. Mateer also works in the real estate industry, specializing in residential and lifestyle properties in New Zealand's winterless far north.

Her two daughters and four grandsons live in the United States and are a constant inspiration for many of her stories.

OTHER TITLES BY LEONIE MATEER:

Business:

The Caboodles Blueprint – Turn Your Idea into Millions

Have a Product Idea? – How Many Could You Sell? – a collection of business articles.

Health and wellbeing:

Psoriasis – The Simple Cure – Who Knew?

Psoriasis - Staying Clear - The Healthy Alternative – a must read for any psoriasis sufferer.

Fiction:

"The Audrey Murders" – a seven book series starring Audrey Wetherby, a serial killer living in idyllic small towns in New Zealand.

Children's fiction:

The Magical World of Dantonia

Black Lake

The Bird Boys

Mason's Secret

Tarot Card Online Game

www.readyourownfortune.com

A do-it-yourself game that enables players to read their own fortunes online, anytime, anywhere. Her sixty-three-card deck, based on ancient fortune telling cards, has been deciphered with the assistance of professional psychics.